Saving Deets!

ZACK GONZALEZ

Saving Deets!

A Family's Journey with Autism

Tafford Publishing

Trafford Publishing ®

Trafford 1663 Liberty Drive

Bloomington, IN 47403

www.trafford.com

Gonzalez, Zack, 1993–

Saving deets!: a family's journey with autism / by Zack Gonzalez

1. Special Needs. 2. Autism 3. Parenting and Families. 4. Title

ISBN:978-1-4269-1762-2 (sc)

First printing, October 2009

Printed in the United States

Cover Design by Alison Holen

Cover Photo by Gloria Sule & Leon Shultz-Ray

This book is dedicated to all the families out there with a voice. Recovery is possible and I hope this book motivates you to never give up and always speak up.

Deets:

You are my inspiration and I love your with all my heart. I will always fight for you. Thank you for helping me find me voice again. Together we will conquer the world, one step at a time.

Special Thanks To:

Ethan, for being my inspiration,

My family for always supporting me and always
believing in me,

And Especially to

Mom for never letting me give up,

Dad for always reminding me that the Lord is
always on my side.

Also to

The amazing Walk Now and Play Now Committee
for being such an awesome and supportive team,

And Lastly to

The families that shared their stories in this book,
you have helped make a difference.

Contents

Preface

What is a Deets?

I'm sure many of you are wondering what the heck a Deets is? Fist of all, Deets is my brother, not a thing. His name is Ethan but we call him Deets. My other brother EJ gave him the name Deets while on our road trip to Washington. Ethan was looking out the window and EJ kept yelling at him "Deetens!...No Deetens!" and really ever since then, Ethan became Deetens and then we shortened it to Deets. Throughout the book you will notice that I will use both Ethan and Deets but I am referring to the same person; I'm not talking about two different people.

Saving Deets?

The title, *Saving Deets!,* can be a little misleading. Many people may misinterpret what I mean by "*Saving Deets*" but here it is: This book is basically my family's journey on accepting and recovering Ethan, as well as, making a difference in the autism society. It is pretty much our way of "saving" him. Saving him from all the negativity and neglect. Saving him from the ignorance and ignorant people. Saving him from the deadly toxins in our environment. Saving him from the physicians that are giving him these toxins from these vaccines and somewhat saving him from autism.

What is Autism & Why Am I So Passionate About It?

Autism is a neurological disorder that a child can be diagnosed with around the age of three and lasts throughout their entire life. It is a part of the autism spectrum disorder (ASD). There are many forms of ASD; ranging from high-functioning to severe.

Today in 2010, one in every 150 children is diagnosed with autism. Every twenty minutes, another child is diagnosed. Autism is more common than diabetes, cancer, and AIDS combined. It does not discriminate by race or by social group. This disorder makes it difficult for these individuals to communicate socially and verbally. They tend to have repetitive behaviors (such as hand flapping and spinning) and some have forms of OCD (Obsessive-Compulsive Disorder). Most of them also tend to have speech problems and have a difficult time with language development and proper usage. My brother Ethan is one of the many that has been diagnosed with autism. Every since he was first diagnosed in 2005, I have been very passionate about the cause. I have attended a large variety of benefit events and charity events that raise money for the cause. I have even created my own event. By writing this book I hope to bring more awareness and get many physicians to see that many of the causes of autism can be due to some neglect on their part.

Is There a Cure or Treatment?

There is no cure for autism but there are many therapies and treatments that have been shown to work in some cases. There are many therapies used by specialists and families that have been proven to work, as well as, diets (such as the GFCF Diet and Special Carbohydrate Diet) that have also been proven by families to work. I talk all about the different treatments that can be used to help recover (NOT CURE) autism. These therapies and diets help these individuals recover from their symptoms and if they are removed or not fully completed then the individual has a possibility of regaining their symptoms.

The Cause of Autism

There are many different beliefs as to what is the cause of autism but really the main cause is unknown. There are scientist and doctors that say that it is solely genetics, though the gene or chromosome that it contains it has not been found. There are also studies that prove that vaccines can have a link to autism but many physicians disagree. The environment may also play a huge role in autism but there is still a lack of research. Personally, I feel that vaccines and toxins in our environment combined are the main cause of autism because most of these children have weak immune systems and with a weak immune systems, these children are unable to process many of these toxins and with help from toxins in vaccines, their immune systems are only weakened. There are chapters about vaccines and the role of the environment included in the book as well as sections where I talk about the neglect from certain physicians.

A Little About Myself

Who am I, you ask? I am a sibling of child with autism. I am also a huge advocate for autism and currently on the committee for the Los Angeles Walk Now for Autism and Play Now for Autism. I am currently enrolled at a local private high school in my neighborhood and will graduate in 2011.

I am very active in the autism community. I have organized and hosted my own charity events and I have made speeches, done radio interviews, and written newspaper articles. I am very proud of the position that I am in. I thank the good Lord every day for helping me get to where I want to be.

A Little More About the Book

The book is told through my point of view with a little help from my mom. I have also hand-picked a few other parents, siblings, and close friends of mine to tell their stories and share their experiences. There are also pictures at the end of each story to help you get a visual of the families and events.

Chapter 1:
Getting Hit by A Train

"Like with any journey, autism brings
you a road unexpected."

- **Nancy Quesada,** Mother of Ethan Quesada, Advocate
for Autism, and Motivational Speaker.

I am going to tell you a story of a little boy. This was a cute chubby little baby boy. He was just like every other newborn. He laughed and he cried and he did everything that we call "normal." He was charming with the sweetest smile. He was such a good baby. He would play on his own and laugh at funny things. He was developing well. Then, he stopped; he had changed and was no longer this happy high-functioning baby. It was like he was taken over by this force that stopped him from proceeding. He went from this perky baby to this baby that just sat there. It was clear that something happened and this is where that walk on the railroad tracks had begun.

The more he decreased the closer that train came and finally, it hit! He was diagnosed with autism. When I found this out, I was in shock. I had no idea what it was and why it was happening. Then, before I realized it, this story that I was telling you about this innocent little boy became the story of my brother. My brother Ethan, AKA "Deets."

Deets was this little boy, and this was his story and how he started to grow and how we all started to grow in loving him and helping him learn. We were all shocked and some of us were pretty scared because now we had to really dedicate all of our time to him. It was tough but we all pushed through it and started on this new journey. Our lives have definitely been changed. Most people see it as a curse or a form of bad karma, but I see it as a stepping-stone to help us grow and become stronger. Autism does not have to be this bad thing that people make it out to be. I see it as a message from

God. God is trying to tell us something; he is trying to send us a message and that message is this crazy train that just hit us. It is the message that we have to unravel and read, and use it to change this fallen world, one step at a time.

LEARNING TO ACCEPT IT

After finding out that Ethan was autistic, I was a bit scared and a bit jealous. He was getting all the attention and all the focus was on him. The sibling rivalry had begun for all three of us. I was so used to getting all the attention and when he came around, I didn't know how to react. It was tough to sit in the sidelines and just watch as he took the lead. It was all about making sure we had a close eye on him and making sure he makes it to therapy on time. There was so much going on, it was overwhelming.

Then, I started to think and I started to research. I went online and tried to find out what autism spectrum disorder is. I never really understood what it was at first and I never really knew how to accept it but eventually I grew to see that it was not going change. Ethan is autistic and it was going to stay that way, whether I liked it or not.

Autism is a disorder that I have to live with even though I didn't have it. It was hard trying to make sure he did not run off in the super market and making sure he was always holding someone's hand. None of us were prepared for this, but it happened. We were all on this new path together and we just had to go along with it. I would always just sit there and wonder why this happened to me. I was so selfish and I did not even see it. All I wanted was for it to be easier and less tiring. I just wanted to live my same old life again. I wanted to have a brother that did not need so much attention.

After a while, it got boring sitting there feeling sorry for myself, so I stood up and once again went back to that computer and did some research and really started to get deep into what autism is. I dug and dug and never really found an answer that was to my standards. I saw autism as a bad thing, and really it wasn't that it was a bad thing; it was that I saw it in a bad way. My mother taught me that when we see things as negative, then they will always be negative until we make them positive. We have the power to control our lives; we have free will, we just need to know how to use it. We need to learn how to not be a victim of circumstances and instead be a person of power and in control of our lives. I believe that we are not controlled by destiny, but we are all destined to do something. God made us individually and he made us with a plan set. He put us on this earth for a reason.

A Whole New Mind-Set

I started to change my mentality and tried to see the good in autism. I never found the good in it but I did find that by changing the way I looked at it that it had become something that was no longer bad. So now I was even more confused, I didn't see it as bad but I still never found out how it is good. So I still sat there scratching my head wondering what the hell it is. Then I found out that I was spending too much time trying to search for an answer that I wasn't going to find because the answer that I was searching for was ideal. It was an answer only suitable to me. So then I started to ask myself, "Now what?" I did not see that I was supposed to help my brother and not just find a scientific definition. I should have been helping him all along but instead I was still only thinking of myself.

After coming to this obvious conclusion I started to think yet again. I starting thinking of how I can help him and what methods we could use to cure him. I was all for curing him and getting rid of the disorder. I saw it as a problem that needed a solution. I learned that not everything thing that I did not agree with is a problem and not everything needs a solution. I saw that this little boy with autism is my brother and it is my job, as his big brother, to help him and to accept him. The key word is acceptance. It is the word that is far from our minds at first but the answer that we are searching for.

Acceptance is Key

Acceptance is key. It is the next step that helps us move on and help the children improve. It is the beginning of a whole new journey. This new journey is all about helping. We have to help these children and get the world to see that they may not act like every other child but overall they are just kids and really aren't that different. And besides, no two individuals are alike. We all have differences and special gifts. They are just children and treating them differently and making fun of them is just cruel. We have to make a stand and fight for them. We are their voice; if they cannot speak then we must speak for them. It is our job to take a stand and give them that power. We need to educate them and find ways to help them. The first step is always accepting them. Once we accept them as they are, then we can help them become the strong individuals we want them to be.

Ethan is who he is and I cannot change that. I wanted change for him but really the change needed to come from me. I needed to change the way I was acting and accept that he was going to be who he is. Once I realized that, I was onto a whole new track. It is very difficult to look in the mirror and say that you need to change especially when you are as stubborn as I am. It was very hard but as soon as I admitted to myself that he was not different, I saw how special this little boy is. I saw his potential and the effort that I needed to make to help him continue on that path to greatness.

Chapter 2:
My Son Has
Autism

"Love your kid. Love your partner. The kid is not defined by a diagnosis. He is still a kid."

- **Priscilla Picard**, Mother of Zach Picard and Advocate for Autism.

N ow honestly, I can only tell you what I know and since I was only around eleven years old when Ethan was diagnosed back in 2005, I cannot tell you much about that part but I do know someone who can. This is one person that I love dearly and I was dying to figure out how I can get her to write a piece for this book. She is really the only one that knows what really happened and it was not until I was reading *Louder Than Words* by Jenny McCarthy (the chapter where she finds out her son has autism) when I figured out how to fit her in this book. Nancy Quesada is such an awesome person and I love her so much! How could I not? She's my mother! Here she is to tell the story of Ethan's early years:

Ethan's Story

By Nancy Quesada

Like with any journey, autism brings you a road unexpected. Maybe it is the way life should be. Ethan continues to give me that unexpected road, every single day. I never know when he will say a new word or act like a "good boy" when I desperately need him to. Was Ethan born autistic? This is the most confusing question I know. At first I thought maybe he was, the signs were just not obvious at first. Then I cannot ignore how he responded to me as a baby. He smiled, laughed, repeated sounds I made, and then he changed. I remember the first sign; clearly there was a change in him at eight months old. He was due for his shots; I schedule to have them done before we went on our two-week road trip. It was Christmas time so we were quite busy with our plans. There was not an immediate change in him, but I found it odd how quiet he was on the road. Elijah, who is one year older than Ethan, fussed over everything. Perfectly understandable for a toddler who is sitting strapped in a car seat for long hours. Not Ethan, he was quiet, calm, and a little zombie-like I thought. It did not matter, he was good and we were on a trip. I did not understand it then but I had this uneasy feeling Ethan was just too calm.

Kinda funny how both out stories start off the same. Except for the fact that I didn't mention the road trip. A little FYI, it was on this road trip that EJ (Elijah) first called Ethan Deetens, which eventually grew into Deets.

On our way home Ethan's emotion remained pretty much the same, until he let out the loudest scream I have ever heard. We all jumped out of our seats and to his assistance. Obviously something was bothering him. As I turned back to see what might be the problem, I was surprised to find him calm, zoned-out and staring out the car window. Strange, I thought, but he looked fine, there was no sign of an uncomfortable feeling. We continued to drive and about an hour later Ethan screamed again. As before we jumped to his aid. Again, his eyes were out the window, and no expression from his face. We all had the same attitude: "I guess he's fine." My gut feeling felt otherwise, a mother always knows. In the next sixteen hours we drove, Ethan screamed about ten more times. Each time we tried something different in figuring what could be disturbing him. Since Ethan was always a good baby it was easy to assume he was fine. I just could not avoid the idea there was something definitely different, something unusual.

As the days passed I began to notice other things. He was fascinated with Disney computer-animated movies; he would sit and zone-in for an entire movie. Yet he showed no interest in baby movies or cartoons. Then, there was the no response period. I thought, just five months ago he turned when we called his name, now he seemed uninterested. I also saw how intriguing a toy car of any type was to him. He enjoyed starring at the ceiling fan, and finally the deaf assumption. Every mother I know touched by autism knows this question, "Is he deaf?" Being deaf just did not make sense. How can he not hear, when a truck or loud car drove by the house he would race to the window to see it pass by?

When Ethan turned one I felt a need to figure him out. I arrived from work to pick him up at my mother-in-laws house. He was zoned into the television. I walked beside him and called "Ethan," no response. Why would he not care to see me? "Ethan, let's go home," no response. Is he deaf, again I questioned. My thoughts began to run ahead of me; I was determined to find it out once and for all. I remember the movie, *Mr. Holland's Opus*, the part when the mother gets pots and pans to know if her son can hear. I ran to the kitchen, pulled out two large pots and stood right behind Ethan. First, I banged softly, no response, then, a bit louder, nothing. I stomped my foot, maybe the vibration will get his attention, then again, nothing. How I knew this at that moment I will never know, but I looked at him and said, "Oh God, he has autism."

The next day I called our pediatrician to make an appointment. The receptionist told me our doctor was out of the office and suggested I leave her a message. I thought to myself, "I need to talk to her." I needed her to tell me I was just over reacting. I did not want to say out loud, "I believe my son has autism," which might not get her attention. As her voicemail beeped to allow my message, my cracked, desperate voice said "Doctor, my son is deaf. I need you to see him right away." That same day the office called back and I had an appointment for the next day.

Ethan and I arrived at the doctor's office. How do I tell Dr. Levinson I lied over the phone? I know Ethan is not deaf. As I sat in the waiting room looking at Ethan I thought, "what if he is deaf?" That immediate thought strangely brought me a hint of relief. We were called in and I was open to any diagnoses Dr. Levinson gave us, I can handle anything. The door opened, she looked different. Her eyes were swollen and a feeling of sadness followed. "Forgive me for being late, my mother is dying, I was not going to come in, but hearing your message I felt I needed to be here." I felt a little bad, not only did she make time for me but also I lied to her. Truth is, I wanted my lie to be true. "Doctor, my son is not deaf, he has autism. I just know it." I held a firm look to her eyes. As she examined Ethan I explained his obsession with cars, spinning, and hand flapping. His no eye contact and disconnection to his surroundings was evident. It did not take much time when she gave me that look. She had eyes of a mother, her sadness gained strength over me. "I think you are right, it could not be anything other than autism." I stood there frozen; she looked as if she wanted to cry for me. I couldn't cry, there was no more emotion left in me. "Okay Doctor, what is my next step?" She gave me phone numbers, information, regional center. She went on about therapies, doctors, advocates; it was all a blur, too much to take in. I picked up Ethan, gave her my deepest condolences for her mother, and walk to what felt like the twilight zone.

When I got home, I sat on the couch hoping for a solution. I sat there alone. I needed someone at that moment. I called Jay, my husband, and with one sentence "The doctor says Ethan has autism." He left work and came home. How do I make this okay? Or how can I cover this up? I did not want anyone to know.

The more I have tried to learn about autism and Ethan, the more I learned about life. Ethan brings me great joy. Often I have felt guilty that he has given me so much more than I have given him. Life is different for me now; I appreciate the tiniest things. The joys of this world are not what they use to be. A friend once told me "You have every right to complain, there is a lot on your plate." That friend, although meant well, was wrong. How can I complain about a gift? Ethan has taught me to live in the moment; he does not fuss about the past, nor worries about the future. He just is. People often say that there is a light, which beams from an autistic child's eyes. I believe that light comes from the ability to be completely present. Which is exactly what they are "a gift."

Saving Deets!

Ethan & Mommy's Birthday! (March 8 & 9)

Zack Gonzalez

Please note that some of the names in this chapter have been changed or modified for protection purposes

Saving Deets!

Chapter 3:
Autie-Dads

"In any man's life, or person for that case, one is always surprised by how many words can dramatically change your life. In a father's life the first example of this is when you hear those four little words, 'You're having a son!'"

- **Salvador Medrano**, Father of Quinn Medrano and Advocate for Autism

Many times we hear of the moms going out there and finding different methods and diets to try and help their children and really the question is, "Where the hell are the dads at?" There are too many dads that are just sitting around on their lazy asses not doing anything leaving the mothers to fend for the children themselves. It has been proven that a marriage is more likely to fail if the couple has a special needs child. Hmm…I wonder why?! There are so many moms that I have heard say that if it weren't for the financial security of their husbands, they would be gone. The only reason they are still married is because their child needs constant one-on-one attention and it disables them from working so they rely on their husband's paycheck. It is sad to hear and read these stories and statistics. These dads should be out there helping to defeat autism and put in just as much effort as the moms.

Not all dads are like this though and I am glad to say that Ethan's dad is *almost* the complete opposite. He is beside my mom 100 percent. Now, he's not going out and doing a bunch of research and advocating as much but he does listen to my mom and know that sometimes she may know best. He is a true "Autie-Daddy[1]." I can tell that he really wants to see Ethan do much better.

My mom loves to travel! We have gone from state to state in the U.S. but she's gone even farther. Now, when she leaves, obviously she cannot take Deets with he because he has school and therapy but she always leaves him in the best care: with Amber and

---

[1] An Autism Father

Jay. Amber is my mom's sister (my aunt) and Jay is my mom's husband (my step-dad; EJ & Deets' dad). Jay and Amber do not always get along but without my mom there, they both need to bump it up and work just a little harder to take care of Deets and make sure that he eats only what he is allowed to, being that he's on the GFCF Diet.

Aside from Jay, there was another dad that I thought would qualify great for this chapter his name is Salvador. He is one of the great friends I have met through Autism Speaks and Walk Now. I thought that he has been an amazing example and that he deserves to share his story through a father's perspective. Here is his story:

Four Small Words

By Salvador Medrano

In any man's life, or person for that case, one is always surprised by how many words can dramatically change your life. In a father's life the first example of this is when you hear those four little words, "You're having a son!" Not to say there is anything wrong with having a girl (even now after three boys I still secretly still want one), but there is a certain resonance as a man in having a boy. Dreams of shaping a starting shortstop for the New York Yankees, the old school point guard for the Lakers, or even lead guitar player in an up-and-coming band seem to dance in your head. And such was my pre-birth joy about the newly named Quinn.

One of the greatest tragedies of my life was that I was not present for Quinn's birth, a tale better told at some other point, but suffice it to say it hurt me deeply. During the course of his first few days on this planet, it included a triple digit fever and the possibility of a spinal tap. His mother handled it beautifully and after five days I was finally able to hold my baby boy. He looked like me, smelled like me, and loved like me. Seriously, there was just a fundamental change on how I viewed the world and it was this little creature that had totally turned me inside out.

So, life continued beautifully for the next two-and-a-half years, including the birth of his brother, Soren, and all was proceeding as planned. Quinn astounded us with his intelligence, including the ability to start reciting and identifying the ABC's at a little over a year old. Though I thought he would start for the UCLA men's basketball team, maybe he was destined to be a professor there instead. The possibilities were endless and his story was already being written.

Then, suddenly it all started to fall away. Quinn became less outgoing; he wasn't talking as much. He started to focus on certain things, most noticeably cars. This included lining them up, on our rather ample coffee table, as if they were in a parking lot. His language consisted of pointing at words in magazines and parking lots and identifying them by logo. Most distressful to his mother, he would not look her in the eye and hold a gaze and the worst: he still had not said "I love you mama," like many three year olds we knew.

At this point I must give her all the credit; had it not been for my wife's insistence that something was wrong, I probably would not have gotten Quinn an intervention as early as we did. I mean really, in my head he was a little quirky, sure, but something wrong with him? No way. I mean not all men are good talkers. So what if I had one of the silent types? It'd be okay; he'd shake it off and be totally cool at age five when he had to start kindergarten.

It is at this point that I got the second set of four words that changed my life: "Your son is autistic." I can still remember the day. It was a couple of months after his first birthday on a really nice early autumn afternoon. After having been told by our school district to take him to our local regional center to have him tested, we thought we were ready for anything. Then the doctor sat us down and said those words. It's amazing what happens at times like this. I have rarely been shocked in my life, but damn if that wasn't one of them. We must not have said anything for a while as I remember the doctor asking us if we needed a minute, which we responded to in the negative. No way were we going to show this doctor any weakness. I remember we talked about some of the services available for him, but honestly he could have been speaking German because I was in such shock, I didn't hear a word he said. It was like constantly being out of breath but having to breathe. There honestly was not a lot of oxygen going to my brain at that point.

We then stumbled out the office. I remember we didn't talk much on the way to our cars. I think we were both in such shock. I actually went back to work and finished off my day. I clearly remember going to Barnes and Noble and getting just about every book I could find on the subject with the idea that I was somehow going to cure or fix Quinn. I also remember calling my brother in the parking lot and finally just breaking down. I have very rarely, if ever, sobbed that way. You know the kind of crying that kind of lifts you off your seat. But damn if I didn't do it that night in that Barnes and Noble parking lot. I collected myself and went home to comfort Quinn's grieving mother. Then, we did what we learned to do so many times after that: dusted our selves off, got back on the horse, and started working on how we could make Quinn's life a little easier and a lot better.

That was seven years ago and though I'd love to say that we lived happily ever after, but we didn't start our tale with the word "Once upon a time…" Since then, Quinn has another brother (Julian, which was really good) and his mother and I have divorced (that on the other hand was really bad). Quinn has gone through the ups and downs associated with the condition, which in the end has settled at a high-functioning autism. He does talk now and even attends a mainstream school, plays on a typical basketball team (and just scored a basket), is a part of a Cub Scout pack, and even sings in his church choir. We are all amazed with his progress and bravery.

That being said, as is usually the case with his part of the spectrum, new challenges have cropped up. Being in 3rd grade and now almost ten and he is starting to recognize that he is different from the rest of the boys in his class and he has had some difficulties adjusting. Though he feels as if he doesn't have friends, his younger brother reports that he is actually a part of the kickball group that has formed during recess and is an active and well-respected participant. I actually had one of those stomach-punching moments recently when he announced he was sick and tired of being autistic and was wondering at what age it went away. His demeanor has also gotten "darker" and we are well aware of the high rate of depression and suicide amongst high functioning/Asperger Syndrome teenagers. We hope through the love of us and his extended family (as well as some personal counseling) that we will once again meet and beat this challenge.

With that, it brings me to the final four words of my story, "My son is autistic." I am proud of that because it has brought so many things in my life that I may have never known I had or needed. It has made me a better father, not only to Quinn but to his brothers as well. It has made me a better parent, as I have newfound patience and understanding, which I don't think I'd have if it was not for this special blessing. And it's made me a better person in so many ways that I would just bore you with the list. Suffice it to say, it's not so much any four words anymore but in fact what emotions they in invoke within you. As for me, "My son is autistic" now only invokes nothing but love. I Love You Quinn!

Salvador had a very touching story. Another man that I thought would qualify as an Autie-dad is Mr. Phillip Hain.

Here is Phillip to tell his story of his involvement in the autism community and his son's life:

The Tale of the Hain Family

By Phillip Hain

I must admit that I don't remember the exact date. That's not a horrible thing, but so many people I've met over the years remember it so distinctly. It was sometime in May of 1996. I do remember it had been a bad day at work; little did I know that it was not going to get any better. And I do recall that the traffic was really nasty because there was an accident on the freeway and I was late to the appointment.

But I remember the words very clearly as the therapist said them. "Andrew has Asperger's Syndrome." The first reaction that went through my mind was, "Well at least it's not autism." Gee, wasn't I naïve. A few months later, the next diagnosis was autism. And so was the third. My wife and I weren't in denial. We just needed to understand what was happening with our son, and what we could do about it.

Even before that day, I remember my first suspicions came when I compared Andrew to other kids I noticed in airports when I traveled. They did simple things that he didn't. More words. More activity. More interaction. More conversation. Something was different, but we didn't know what. Everything could be explained away so easily.

When Andrew wasn't interested in circle time at Gymboree, another parent said, "It took so long for my son to want to sit and participate. Don't worry, he'll grow into it." If only it had been that easy. His love of constantly bouncing on the trampoline was no indication at that point. Wanting to turn every page in the TV Guide should have been an easy giveaway. Being entranced watching the credits at the end of a television program. Able to keep himself amused and not needing attention was nice since it gave us time to relax. Oh, the things we learn. And what we've learned over the past thirteen years. And how it's changed our lives.

I do remember very clearly when the cycle started. It was the day after Thanksgiving 1995 and my parents and my wife's parents said they needed to talk to us. That was very odd, since we all had just spent the holiday together. (I love my parents dearly, but I just saw them the day before). I didn't know exactly what they wanted to discuss, but I had a suspicion that it had to be about Andrew. What else did both sets of parents need to talk with us about?

It must have been very difficult and painful for them to gently try and tell their children that they suspected there was a problem with their grandchild. I have to thank them for having that courage, since they didn't know how we would react, and denial is sometimes very strong. But they didn't know what it was any more than we did, only that he wasn't playing with his cousins and seemed to ignore them.

The numbers have increased so much in the past dozen years, as have both the prevalence and people who know about it. It's strange to think that back then what we take for granted today— that everyone knows about autism—was not everywhere you looked.

Because Andrew had been at home with a nanny, his pediatrician's suggestion was to put him in preschool so he could get more interaction and socialization with other children. It brought on our next challenge—how to get your three year old child into a preschool when he's not potty trained? That certainly limited our options.

When Andrew was diagnosed with autism I talked to a friend who was going through some marital problems. Her husband had disappeared, leaving her to raise their daughter alone. I said to her, "Life has thrown both of us a major curveball that we never could have expected. We have no choice but to deal with it. It probably won't be easy, but that's what we have to do". It hasn't been easy, but it has changed me. It has caused me to become a more involved father, and find inner strength that I never knew I had.

It's difficult to speculate what our lives would be like if Andrew had not been diagnosed with autism. My wife might still be working full time outside the home. I think that my son would have gone to school and I would have attended Back to School Night and Open House. Our involvement with the school, the district, and the educational system would have been very limited. But when you have a child with special needs and learn the terminology, acronyms, and challenges that face parents who deal with Special Education, circumstances take you down another path. Most dads don't know what the letters "IEP" mean or have any need to learn the inner workings of the educational system.

There was the Father's Day when I sat and watched my son playing pinball on the computer. Part of me said that he should be interacting with another person and not playing on the computer. But the other part of me watched him play the game and marvel at his progress. When Andrew first played pinball on the computer the ball kept going down the center and his scores were very low. Progress is when I would marvel at his high score and be amazed at how his hand/eye coordination improved.

What is different being the parent of a child with a disability? We have different levels of accomplishment in which we take pride. Most of our kids are not going to finish at the top of their class or be elected school president. They probably aren't going to be the most popular or have the largest group of friends. And sometimes our kids have to work harder. My wife and I are thankful that Andrew has been included in a regular classroom since kindergarten. Andrew was selected Student of the Month twice during his years in elementary school. Some typical kids never receive that honor. Andrew won the spelling bee for his entire school in 8th grade. Perhaps that is bragging, but it's more to make the point that kids on the autism spectrum can do incredible things.

And we have other reasons to celebrate. I think of the progress he made years ago on his softball team. When he started he could barely swing the bat and connect with the ball. Then he held the bat better and hit the ball off the "T" stand. That was improvement. He then got to where he could hit a ball pitched to him and get to first base. In the final game of one season he fielded a ground ball and threw it to a teammate. It's all about progress, just measured on a different scale.

Andrew really loves music and enjoys singing. There are not many kids—with autism or typically developing—who can say they've sung on stage with a Grammy award-winning singer. And he's done just that: twice.

Having a child with a special need has taken me on a journey I never imagined. I don't know if it has made me a "better" person, but I wouldn't be the same without Andrew having autism. I've learned to become more of a fighter. When Andrew was first diagnosed, someone said that my wife and I would have to learn how to advocate for him and make sure he got what he needs. At the time I had no idea what that meant. Now I look back and realize what I was being told. It's made me appreciate the teachers, social skills group leaders, case workers, and other parents who have helped give Andrew what he needs.

Being the parent of a child with a disability, you learn even more to expect the unexpected. Everyone wonders what will happen to their kids and what will they be when they grow up, but those concerns are magnified so much more. It's not whether your kid will be a doctor, teacher. or firefighter. It's whether he will be able to get a job and live on his own. My wife and I wonder, "Will he be able to survive when we're not around?" Most parents of typically developing children have never heard of a Special Needs Trust.

Many years back, I saw a television commercial for one of those true life police shows where they re-enact dramatic moments in people's lives. The episode being promoted was about a little boy whose mom got hurt very badly at home. He was probably three years old and he dialed 911 all by himself. His mom was saved. It was good for them, but at that point in our lives, we didn't know what was going on with Andrew. I remember thinking, "I don't know if my son will ever be able to dial 911, let alone have a telephone conversation." So much has changed since then.

Sometimes when I hear Andrew talk, the clarity in his thoughts seems to be unreal. I wonder what is going on inside his brain. And I have to snicker to myself, thinking back years ago about the psychiatrist who suspected mental retardation and never said the word "autism". It takes restraint to not walk back into his office and show him Andrew's test scores in math and spelling. The things Andrew says are so vivid, but often disconnected to his surroundings.

Andrew knows the most obscure facts about television game shows. He can tell us the date we went to a taping of "Wheel of Fortune" ten years ago and what the answer was to the bonus round puzzle. There are times when he's watching that show at home and yelling the answer at the television set, while the contestant on the screen is struggling. Andrew remembers the name of the street where we stayed in a hotel in Canada while vacationing there over eight years ago.

Part of me is amazed at how bright he is and how his mind works. And I wonder and worry how this will serve him as an adult. I feel fortunate that he has an engaging personality and that people like him. But will these traits that made him likeable at thirteen help him when he's twenty-two? Although he is friendly, he doesn't have real friends. I describe him as socially indifferent, recognizing the feelings and personalities of others, but perfectly content to be by himself.

In thinking about past struggles, our concerns, and the things he has accomplished, the culmination of everything had to be Andrew's Bar Mitzvah. There is a synagogue not too far from us which has a program for special needs children. Knowing that we wanted Andrew to have a Jewish education, my wife and I enrolled him there for kindergarten. As he made progress in his regular school and we prepared for a full inclusion program with typically developing kids, it only made sense that we should try to put him in the same type of learning environment for religious school.

So we left that synagogue and joined one closer to our home. They didn't have any program designed for kids with special needs, but we were not worried. It worked out fine when the teachers said he listened, didn't socialize much with his classmates (no surprise), wasn't disruptive, occasionally asked questions, and was doing about the same as the other kids.

When he got to 4th grade we decided to start him in Hebrew School. Because he had started reading at an early age, we were not concerned that learning another language would be a problem or confusing to him. The weekday Hebrew teachers had the same type of progress reports as the Religious School teachers. It helped that we attended Friday night Shabbat services on a fairly regular basis. Because Andrew has a good memory, his mere presence at services had an effect and everything was penetrating his mind. The prayers and melodies resonated inside him, but we didn't know to what extent.

Andrew also had to learn his particular Torah portion in Hebrew, and that involved both words and the associated melodies. He studied each week with the Cantor of our synagogue, who wasn't worried and said that he would be ready when the appointed day arrived. He practiced daily and—from what I could hear—was on key and sounding good. I helped him with the talk he had to give that explained what he read and how it applied to his life. He also said he wasn't nervous about the impending event. My own personal hope was for him to do a good job, and for the people attending to have a fun time and appreciate the religious significance of the ceremony, regardless of whether or not they were Jewish and could understand Hebrew.

Andrew led a very nice service and chanted his portion very well. He giggled a few times during his speech, but managed to regain his composure. The audience laughed with him and seemed to enjoy the fact that he was just being himself. There wasn't any pretension. The Rabbi must have thought he did well because he joked that Andrew could be his substitute when he took vacation. I wasn't able to comprehend how people reacted to him until the reception which followed.

Every parent wants his child to do a good job, but the comments and praise were astounding. To say that people gushed and were in awe would not be an overstatement. Several said it was one of the most spiritually uplifting Bar Mitzvah ceremonies they had ever attended. There was some indefinable quality that raised it to a level far above anyone's expectations. The words we heard were "amazing," "fantastic," "hard to top," "one for the record books" and "perfect." He even created a buzz within the congregation.

For days and weeks after the ceremony, people who attended repeatedly told us how much they enjoyed themselves. People who had not been there said they heard what a great job he had done and were sorry they missed it. I was overjoyed to hear it all because I felt that he had given a wonderful gift to everyone else. For a boy who had been so echolalic at age three to be able to do what he did was not exactly a miracle, but it certainly was emotional and inspiring beyond my imagination.

Andrew still has his challenges in school with understanding what he is reading. That night he talked about how God is present in his life and what it meant to him. There was something almost magical the way he touched so many people that evening. Like many other children with autism, in some ways he is very simple in his approach to the world around him. But it was clear that night there is so much going on in his head that the rest of us won't understand. In his own unique way, he gets it.

Of all the changes Andrew has inspired, perhaps the biggest one was in my career. It used to be that my day job was working in marketing and my night job was volunteering for an autism organization. The former was my profession and the latter was my passion.

Two years ago I applied for a full time position with Autism Speaks as the Executive Director of the Los Angeles chapter. My job at the time was content but it didn't create anything inspiring within me. I wore an autism pin to work every day because I always wanted people to ask me about it. My boss and co-workers knew how I spent my free time. When I was going through the interview process I had very conflicting feelings because there was the usual amount of safety in staying with the existing job that contrasted with the excitement (and uncertainty) of embarking on something new.

With each phase as I advanced to the next level I wanted to make sure I was doing the right thing. Of course the irony is that the only person who could reassure me of that was me. As the timing of the final selection approached I was about to go on vacation to Europe so I left without knowing what the decision would be.

It was the evening of the day Andrew and I arrived in London when I called home and my wife said, "Congratulations. You got the job." After I recovered from the shock of hearing those words, I vacillated in the feelings of fear and euphoria. Fortunately the fear subsided very quickly. I knew the challenge of trying something completely different that lay ahead, and deep inside felt the satisfaction that I had absolutely made the right choice.

Since the day I started it's been amazingly fulfilling. I wasn't sure how the transition from volunteer to staff member would be but it's been so rewarding. I've joked on occasion that I'm less credible now that I get paid to talk about autism, but the advantage is that I can do it all the time—not just in my "off" hours. I also say that I've turned my former night job into my day and night job. I wouldn't have it any other way.

There are times when I have to stop and wonder when I'm saying something if at a particular moment I'm speaking as a parent or employee because there are definitely occasions when the two overlap. But that doesn't matter as much as knowing that I'm making a difference. I tell that to people all the time and it's so true. It's sometimes depressing and frustrating when we have to delve into the political side of autism but I know deep down that everyone is passionate about what they believe in, and we all want to make a difference.

I know for myself that it's not just for my son, but the millions of other kids and adults who face challenges and also have tremendous success stories to tell. Their difficulties, setbacks, accomplishments and success stories inspire us with the hope and willpower to keep fighting and never give up.

Saving Deets!

Chapter 4:
Siblings

"The most important thing you can do is help your peers accept and appreciate those different from them in hopes of increasing acceptance and decreasing ignorance and stigma!!"

- **Svetlana G. Ravinovich**, Psy.D., Sister of Roshel Sheina Gerzon

Zack Gonzalez

This is the chapter that is often left out at times when an autistic child comes into the family. I know this through experience. It is bad enough to have a new baby brother or sister join the family and get all the attention being the baby. However, it is even worse when that baby brother or sister is autistic. Not only is the attention being taken away but then the extra responsibility is also assumed on to the siblings.

Once the siblings get the green in their eyes it's heading toward a whole new level of sibling rivalry. Luckily for me, I did not have to endure too much of that. By the time Ethan was born I already had one sibling from my mom's side: Elijah (EJ), and two from my dad's: Shawn and Isaiah (followed by Breanne, Ethan, and Joshua). I am the oldest so I was already used to living with additional children and kind of having to share that attention. When Ethan arrived I already had an idea of what to expect, or at least I though I did.

The good thing about it is that my mother had me when she was young, so growing up every time she went somewhere I would obviously go too. So ever since I was a baby, I was always around adults and people older than me so I already had that older mentality. Even though I have cousins that I would see occasionally, I was still more comfortable being around elders. My maturity level was obviously a bit higher than the "typical" kids my age (or at least that's what I've always been told). The sibling rivalry was not a major issue for me but I did get jealous at times and I did feel left out a bit.

The one that did have a big issue with Ethan getting a lot of attention was EJ. He had what we call "middle child syndrome." It could be that he was the middle child or that he and Deets were so close in age. He is always fighting with Deets and pissing him off. He just loves to really push his limits and see how far he can get.

To help me tell a little more about what a sibling goes through when they live with an autistic child, I have brought in another sibling. Her name is Lani and she has an autistic sister. It is the pretty much like a flip side. Instead of a big brother telling the story of his younger autistic brother, it's a big sister telling the story of her younger autistic sister.

Here is Lani's story:

That Sister-Sister Bond...

By Svetlana "Lani" Gerzon Ravinovich, Psy.D

November 19, 1996, was the first time I remember telling myself, "This is the happiest day of my life." It was the birth of my sister, Roshel. I hated growing up as an only child and had to wait 14 long years for a sibling. Given the age difference it often felt that my little sister was more like my little daughter. But I always thought that when she grows and we're both adults our age difference won't matter, we'd just be sisters.

I remember the first time I saw her waving her hand close to her eyes as she lay down for a nap, I thought it was odd but didn't think much of it. I wasn't around toddlers and all of my parents' friends' kids were teenagers so everything Roshel did or didn't do was our idea of "normal". It wasn't until a daycare teacher pointed out that Roshel required more individual attention than others, that my mother thought something was wrong. I remember my mother going from doctor to doctor, getting various diagnoses but no guidance as to how to help Roshel. Finally, my mother said she would go back to the Ukraine, which is where my parents and I are from, and find people to help Roshel. To this day, not being a native English speaker, not always knowing how "the system" works poses obstacles for my parents to get the best services possible. I was devastated that my parents would leave and I wouldn't be able to watch my sister grow up. It was merely by accident that I shared my frustrations with my hairstylist who then told me about the legal responsibility of the school district to provide my sister with an appropriate education. This was the day that got the ball rolling.

I was a freshman, pre-med student at UCLA, when I remember sitting in my parents' living room and hearing the heartbreaking news that my sister has autism. No one could really explain to us what it was or how it was going to be treated. The only thing we were told was that this was a life-long disorder. The thought that it would never get better crushed me. At that moment I probably saw my entire life flash by me, and the selfish realization that I would never have what I longed for, a real sister-sister relationship. My parents and I thought she would never be able to feed or dress herself and would have to go live in an institution, because that's what happened to kids with similar presentations in the former Soviet Union. The only way I knew to cope with my grief was to learn about autism and educate my family to help my sister.

I enrolled in Dr. Ivar Lovaas' class at UCLA, learned about applied behavioral analysis, and even got into the work myself. This was most empowering. I loved going to these kids' homes and watching them and their families push themselves everyday to just see a little bit of progress. This was very inspiring and a light at the end of the tunnel. Not speaking the language fluently, my parents always felt as outsiders in various autism support groups. Nevertheless, as moral support for my parents and as my sister's advocate, I continued to drag them to various meetings and attended all school conferences and Individual Education Plans. I enjoyed going to the clinic meetings with Roshel's behavioral providers and hearing the progress she was making. I joined support groups and learned about biomedical interventions and how much they had helped some children with ASD, and went forward in getting Roshel a DAN! doctor and starting her on the DAN! protocol. Unfortunately we saw no improvement in Roshel's language or social skills and we discontinued the treatment.

Apart from making sure that I kept up with the science and relayed all the new information to my parents, what was most important to me was to stay Roshel's sister and not become her therapist. As an undergrad I lived away from home, and traveled back every Saturday to have a sister day with Roshel. That day we would go to Chucky Cheese's or the ice cream shop, or just be silly at home. I knew that if I didn't dedicate time to her she wouldn't care or know who I am.

It's been almost 10 years since Roshel's diagnosis, and life has changed for the better, but there are many more obstacles that lie ahead. I became a Clinical Psychologist, focusing on diagnosis and treatment of individuals with ASD, and other developmental disabilities, and hope to continue learning and soon providing services to adolescents and young adults on the spectrum. I have had the opportunity to meet many wonderful professionals who have helped guide me in the right direction and assist me in eventually becoming the best I can be at helping other individuals like Roshel. I love my job not just because I can help people, but because it is also a means of coping for me with the loss of the sister relationship I wish I had. It has helped me learn to appreciate very basic interactions with Roshel as good enough, and helped me realize that I am so blessed to have her as my sister. It saddens me when I see others around me who have siblings close in age and take their relationship for granted by fighting over negligible things, disrespecting each other in some way, or not showing interest in each other's lives.

Grieving is a life-long process for many, as it is for myself. At important developmental stages and times of transition I am reminded again and again, that I have to accept that Roshel is different and that my relationship with her will never be what I envisioned it to be. As she enters adolescence, this is a trying time for us all, with physical changes, unpredictable behaviors, increasing social demands, and decreasing tolerance and acceptance of her disability and inappropriate behaviors by strangers. She is and will always be my baby sister, who I will care for the rest of my life. She has taught me so much about appreciating the simple things in life, being patient, tolerant and accepting of differences. My hopes and wishes for her are that in her lifetime peers become more accepting of others with whatever challenges they may have, and realize that we were all given a chance at life and should have the opportunity to enjoy it in whatever way it feels joyous to us.

Thank you for taking the time to read about our journey!

Saving Deets!

Zack Gonzalez

It is never a good feeling to be left out which is why parents should really be conscious of their children without special needs. We are your kids, too, and sometimes we don't feel like that. We really do care but we need some attention, too.

Saving Deets!

Chapter 5:
Different Colors
of Autism

"The issue of race has been quite an interesting one."

- **Jeni Zambrano**, Mother of Nico Zambrano and Advocate for Autism

Zack Gonzalez

Now, at this point I thought my book was finally complete after finalizing fifteen chapters but after hearing this extraordinary story of this amazing man that I met through Autism Speaks, I just had to include another chapter. This man's name is Hossein. Hossein is from Iran and he lives here in the U.S. with his family now. He likes to go back to Iran but at times he ends up getting stuck there but no matter what, he makes sure he makes it back to his son. I wanted to touch on the different races. Autism does not discriminate and will hit any race. I asked two people of two different ethnicities to share their stories, struggles, and differences.

Here is Hossein's story:

Hossein's View

By Hossein Mehrabiani

It was the late 1970's. I was studying Civil Engineering in Iran when the revolution started. I was around twenty-three at the time and I wanted to get out of Iran because I didn't agree with the religious views and the dictatorship. I left my country in 1984. They were very strict with the youth and at the time the youth wanted out. I prepared myself to get out of my culture by traveling to different countries. I settled in Argentina in 1987. In Argentina, I stayed for about three and a half years. There I met the love of my life, Gloria. I married her there in Argentina. Argentina was where I spent the most time after I left Iran.

In 1991, we traveled to the United States. I studied some English and tried to adapt to the new cultural and political views. The hardest part was the language. My language is Persian and English and Persian are two very different languages. It was also hard getting a job. I became taxi driver and then did other different things. In late 1991, my first son was born (he is now 18). Then, my son Ebi was born in 1993.

Ever since Ebi was small he was very restless. My mother-in-law came over for a visit and automatically knew that there was something different about him. She urged us to get him checked. We took him to a neurologist. He said that it was obvious that the construction of his brain was not like everyone else's. Though he had no idea what autism is. Later on, Ebi was diagnosed with autism. Gloria and I were shocked. Luckily we were introduced to support groups that helped us.

My family had no idea what autism is. It was difficult explaining it to them since there is no word for autism in Persian. I tried to explain as best as I could but they were pretty accepting. They would send their best wishes and promised to pray for us. They are very supportive.

Though the Iranian culture always out casted those with disabilities. Those that were mentally challenged or disabled were considered crazy. They also try to hide them. It is like they are ashamed. My uncle was diagnosed with schizophrenia and when he would go walking, kids would throw rocks at him. He later died after taking too many medications. It broke my heart when I found out. Especially since I know he was looked down upon by those in Iran. As it is in most third-world countries.

Gloria's family on the other hand was very accepting. I think it was mainly because there was a word for autism in Argentina: autismo. Autism was known about in Argentina. Like I said, Gloria's mother was the one that first noticed that there might be something wrong with Ebi. In 1996, she came over to visit and that's when she noticed Ebi's odd behavior. The Argentinean culture is also more open-minded.

I think that environment was the cause of autism for Ebi. Gloria and I were working hard labor jobs. I was working in construction with a lot of chemicals. I think that it is possible that, that is the reason for Ebi's autism. They didn't catch his autism right away but at the time technology wasn't as great as it is today. I also think it may have been genetic because like I said my uncle was schizophrenic. So there may have been a history of mental disabilities in my family.

If there is one thing that I can ask for, I would just like more awareness. I would also like to see more acceptance. They are not different from us. There is just too much judgment! And it needs to end!

The next story is by Jeni. She is another amazing gal I met through Autism Speaks. She is Asian-America and also was in an interracial marriage. This is her story:

Autism: A Multicultural View

By Jeni Zambrano

As a single Asian-American mom who grew up around Latinos in the Echo Park/Silver Lake area (California), the issue of race has been an interesting one. My half-Mexican-half-Korean son has autism, which for him and I really have not been an issue. Other than some interested queries and looks, friends and strangers have been very accepting of us wherever we go.

Admittedly, I have, on rare occasion, noticed the difficulties that a few first generation Asian families have with disabled children.

Culturally, some Asians from "the old country," though not all, tend to be protective and discreet, and even ashamed or abusive, of their children with disabilities. A small minority of first generation Koreans seem worried society will see their disabled child as taboo. I seem to remember in my studies at UCLA, that in many old cultures throughout history, across races, children with disabilities were viewed upon with fear, and were sometimes completely shut away society or even killed. I wonder if this old fashioned school of thinking still prevails with some people.

But I think this trend changing. Last year, *The Korea Times*, the largest, arguably the most respected Korean newspaper in the world, did an interview with me about this very subject. The writer wanted to totally condemn first generation Koreans about the attitudes of a few families whose kids have autism.

I cautioned him that that was not the right approach. True, there are a few families who believe they have to hide their disabled children from society and keep them sequestered at home. True also, that a few do not even seek intervention for these children, and a very few even abuse them, considering them an inconvenience.

But in my experience, I have seen a flood of first generation Asian families actively love and seek support for themselves and their children through various therapies, diet, and education. So in my mind, first generation Koreans, like everyone else, generally do the very best they can for their autistic kids. I have seen this time and again at my son's therapy centers, their willingness to go past cultural and language difficulties to get their kids the best that the need.

Children of ALL abilities face domestic violence, a lack of resources and abuse around the world, but I am hoping that with continued public awareness and education, we can start to reverse this trend.

I then asked Jeni about her son, Nico's, father. I asked if he was at all in the picture and if their divorce had anything to do with the fact that Nico has autism.

He is only around 2% of the time. He sees him for a few hours twice a week. I wish he could see him more, but he has not made the time. The divorce was for personal reasons, and not related to the autism. Even if Nico was a typical kid, the marriage could not be saved, and he would still not see him more. Sometimes I don't think he was cut out for fatherhood.

Then, since her ex-husband is Latino, I asked her if she would tell me what she experienced with the Latino community and what she witnessed as far as acceptance toward autism.

Latinos rock, I would say most of them have worked hard to help their children, and Ive seen a very small minority who don't think anything is wrong with their kids and don't advocate hard enough. But in general, Latinos really want the best for their kids, and seek it.

Miguel brothers, Nico's tios (uncles) are pretty cool with him. The rest of Miguel's family is still in Mexico, and finances have made it tough to visit them.

I asked how her family took the news about Nico being autistic. By the way, Miguel is Jeni's ex-husband.

My family was fine when they heard about his autism, except my parents at first didn't believe it and were pretty sad at about it. But they came around, and are fine with it now.

In my world, EVERYONE, hands down, has supported my efforts to get Nico help. With the help of Zack's mom, I have been really looking into the GFCF diet.

Saving Deets!

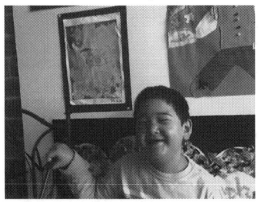

Chapter 6:
Who's to Blame?

"I think that the government or certain public officials in the government have been too quick to dismiss the concerns of these families without studying the population that got sick. I think public health officials have been too quick to dismiss the hypothesis as irrational without sufficient studies of causation."
- **Dr. Bernadine Healy**, former Director of the National Institutes of Health (NIH)

After finding out that Ethan has autism we all were ready to point the finger! It went left and right and back and forth. We never got anywhere blaming each other. It was no use trying to find out who spent the least time with him, who was negligent, who would always watch him. It was pointless! It was stupid and pathetic. We came up with lame excuses and came to dumb conclusions.

It's not worth it to try to blame your family members and friends. All it's going to do is lead to fighting and getting nowhere. All it will do is damage your relationships. We had to think of who else was involved in Ethan's life and what else could be a possibility.

CAN ALL DOCTORS BE TRUSTED?

Ethan's pediatrician seemed nice and trustworthy but was she? She was somewhat good. When my mother first approached her about Deets having autism, she took it into consideration and then agreed that it is autism. She was also very helpful as to leading us to some services and regional centers. Though she did not agree with that fact that the vaccines had an affect on Ethan. Then again what physician would?

Many times our doctors are telling us what to take and what to do. It is rarely a suggestion; more of a demand. And when it's a demand, it's to BUY something that will help us and rarely to take some vitamins or to rest a lot.

They come up with all of these different excuses, symptoms, and medications. It's hard to know if your doctor is telling you the truth. Especially if you see different doctors and they all say it's something different and prescribe a different medication. Funny, huh? We want to believe them and we want to trust them but the question is: Can we?

Not All Physicians and Therapists Are Always Right

When I began advertising for a baseball event I was organizing, I posted an ad on Jen's List[2]. Later the next day a woman wrote into me. Her name was Amalia Starr. She was an author of a book all about hope. Her book is titled *Raising Brandon*. Brandon is her son and he has autism, epilepsy, and other learning disorders. Her book is about how she was told by physicians, school councilors, and therapists that her son would never be able to live on his own and she proved them wrong!

After years of dedication and love, her son recovered. He is now in his 30's and living all on his own. Her story is truly a success story on how she never gave up on her boy. It took her twelve years to complete her book and she is a dear friend of mine to this day. She is so inspirational and I look to her for hope.

She wanted the best for her son and she made it happen! She did not care if she was told that Brandon could never live alone. She had hope and broke through against the predictions. It took her some time but she made it happen.

Jenny is My Idol

Jenny McCarthy is another mother that I look up to. She is a celebrity and she is speaking out. I admire her, Jim Carey (her boyfriend), and her son Evan. They are powerful people that are

---

[2] Jens List is website that lets you know about all the new events and ads that you normally might no find anywhere else. (www.jenlevinson.com).

making a difference. They, too, speak out against the toxins in our vaccines and environment today. They also believe in recovery and a healthy diet. They are many times looked down on for apparently claiming to have "cured autism," but not once have they ever said that autism has been cured. The word they use is "recover," and recover and cure are two different words.

They believe, as do I, that all this shit (like artificial chemicals and preservatives) that these money hungry doctors are telling us to put in our bodies can hurt us. All the drugs and vaccines are just ways to make the pharmaceutical companies more money. Jenny talks all about fight and her success in her books *Louder Than Words, Mother Warriors,* and *Healing and Preventing Autism.*

There are so many other families that are recovering their children, one of then being my own. We are working 100 percent on healing Deets. He is one of the loves of our lives and we will help him no matter what.

Most Doctors Are Like Most Lawyers

You think you can trust your doctor because he or she went to school and they know all their medical terms but really they are just like lawyers; they are just trying to make money. They can lie to you and some can be pretty deceitful. I always thought that it was good to listen to them and take all the medication they would prescribe but really all it was doing was making me high and feel better but in a way that wasn't good. Now I'm not trying to bash doctors at all but seriously they need to care a little more. I am not trying to bash lawyer either. My dad is a lawyer and Amber is going off to law school. I just think that there are too many lawyers and doctors that don't really care about the clients as much as they should.

ADD (Attention Deficit Disorder) and ADHD (Attention Deficit Hyperactivity Disorder) can easily be fixed with a change in diet but instead some people would rather trust their doctors and pay for these pills that "help" them. They might as well be giving them Methamphetamne[3]. It puts them in a trance and makes them believe that they are doing better. Reality is, if I were high and someone said that it would help me focus better I would believe it too, especially coming from a doctor.

All they want is more money. These pharmaceutical companies want more and more because apparently what they are getting is not good enough even if it means our health is at risk. If we really sit and think about it, these doctors are only telling us one-sided information. They tell us the good things about these pills and syrups and we see all the propaganda on the television and we think it's all good. Why don't they put the side effects bigger on the containers or on those commercials or say it slow enough for us to understand what they are saying. And the doctors? Why don't they tell us about ALL the effects of the medications? And if they do, it's either just the minor effects or they say it's no big deal.

I think that it is pretty much a scam to get our money. We go in and we have a headache, they tell us we have some medical condition and give us a bottle of pills to take. We go in and tell them we are not feeling well and they say it is because of this and give us more meds to take. It is sad to see that they think that drugs are the only solution. What happened to Grandma's homemade chicken soup and a little TLC? What happened to eating food that was not filled with toxins and a bunch of other hard-to-pronounce crap? It is a crazy world but we have to be sane and think before we believe everything that these people say. Everything needs to be taken into consideration. Now, I'm no specialist here but some of this information can be pure common sense.

Not All Doctors Are Bad

There are also a lot of good doctors out there that we can trust. The DAN! (Defeating Autism Now!) doctors are some good ones. Defeating Autism Now! is an organization filled with neurological doctors that are here to help. The Autism Research

---

[3] A drug also know as Meth.

Institute founded the organization. They are doctors that believe that you deserve the best and you should not be lied to. They have done studies and research. They have found proof that diets and therapies DO work. They believe in biomedical interventions. They know that there are many families out there that have a voice and have healed children. They have even tried to set up meeting and debates with other physicians to prove to them that vaccines and meds can be hurting us and that diet can work. Though, the other physicians fail to listen. (Hmmm...I wonder why?).

DAN! doctors are some of the few doctors that can be trusted. If you really look deep and search, you can find a good doctor. The NGMDs (New Generation Medical Doctors) are very good as well. They also believe in giving the families a voice. To find a DAN! Doctor or a NGMD near you please go to:

http://generationrescue.com/doctors.html

or

http://www.autism.com/.

VACCINES AND MERCURY

There are exactly thirty-six vaccines that our children are being given. From 1970 to today, it went from ten to thirty-six vaccines. Along with the number of vaccines that increased, that number of children being diagnosed with autism has increased. The number has increase from one in every 10,000 (in the 70's) to one in every 150 in the United States today. It has increased by 6,000 percent, which is CRAZY!

Vaccines Hit Us Hard

Ethan is one of the many that was affected by the vaccines. He was around eight months when he got his shots and we noticed the decrease. He was fine and then he just stopped.

These vaccines are hurting us and have so many toxins in them. We were one of the families that had faith and trusted that the vaccines were good and had to live with the effects of them.

I'm going to tell you right now, they are not always good. They can be helpful to some but they can also greatly damage others. Vaccines were created to help us but instead it is an opposite effect. There are toxins being put into them that are hurting these young infants, with weak immune systems, leaving future defects. Now, like I have said and like I will repeatedly say, I am not a specialist, but I know this by doing research and through personal experience.

Toxins in the Vaccines

One of the toxins is mercury. Thimerosal is a form of mercury. It is one of the neurotoxins in the vaccines. It contains ethyl-mercury. The doses have increased drastically since the 1980's. The rates have gone up like crazy and gone down a bit but some vaccines still contain it. Some being the Hep A/Hep B vaccine, the flu shot, and the Influenza vaccine, just to name a few. The Hep B (Hepatitis B) vaccine was one of the vaccines that was bumped up to being given the day the baby was born. The Hep B vaccine is one of the unnecessary vaccines. It really should only be given if the mother has Hepatitis B.

It is obviously unhealthy to give these babies vaccines that are unnecessary. These babies have a renal system that is not fully developed and the younger they are the harder it is for them to process the mercury, especially if they are born with a weak immune system. It is stupid to give them these shots at such a young age. Sure the doctors say that it is always "better to be safe than sorry," but theses are infants fresh out of their mother's womb that we are talking about. How do these doctors know that they need these vaccines right away? I'm pretty sure they did not run a bunch of test on those babies to find out which ones really need the Hep B vaccine. Once again, it is all a way to make money!

Am I saying to stop vaccinating your kids? No, of course not. I am simply just saying that we need to be very cautious of the vaccines that the children are being given and be aware of the side affects. Though there is no proof that if you spread out the vaccines that it may be healthier, I think it is surely an alternative that should be considered. Doctors DO NOT tell us everything. Some don't even give out the informational sheets about the vaccines. To help you out, I included a few charts on the vaccines. They will tell you all you need to know. There is a whole section of charts on vaccines located toward the end of the book (check the Contents).

Mothers And Mercury

It may be hard to believe but mothers can also be apart of the mercury overload on their children. Some mothers get the flu shots during their pregnancy and the flu shot is one of the vaccines that contain a lot of mercury. Another being the RhoGAM shot. It is another mercury-filled shot that mothers can get during their pregnancy.

Everything that the mother receives and consumes during their pregnancy, goes to the babies and if they consume too much mercury then their babies, too, will get that same toxic overload. Another common mercury-contained substance is the fish consumed by some mothers. If a pregnant woman is not careful and she eats too much fish during her pregnancy then they will also give all that mercury to their child. We must be careful when we eat fish because some contains a lot of unhealthy metals like mercury.

Lastly, the silver fillings in our teeth can also affect these children. This does not just come from the mothers though. Yes, mothers that have fillings can feed that mercury on to the children while they are pregnant but even when the children are older and they get silver fillings that contain mercury, it can affect them.

There are dentists out there that can provide you with mercury-free fillings. They are called mercury-free dentists.

Saving Deets!

You can find a mercury-free dentist by going to http://www.iaomt.org/.

Chapter 7:
The
Environmental
Side

"All illnesses have some hereditary contribution. Genetics loads the gun and environment pulls the trigger."

- **Dr. Francis S. Collins**, Director, National Human Genome Research Institute, National Institutes of Health

I had no idea that the environmental surrounding of an autistic child could actually help the child. Heck, it could even help us!

Home Again

Ever since I was little I would go and visit my dad and my dad's side of the family. I would go over and have a good time. Then, I would be so eager to go back home but once I waved good-bye and walked inside my house I got this weird feeling in my stomach and then I wasn't so glad to be back home. I would get this "ugh, home again" feeling that would make me want to drag my feet. I never understood it. Then, I would walk in to see Amber and my grandma on the couch watching television and then they would ask me how it was visiting my other side of the family. I would respond real nonchalant and just keep on walking and then Amber would make some stupid remark like "Oh great, he went over there and was all goodie-goodie and now he comes home and acts like a brat, again." How could I be happy to be home hearing comments like that? I don't know if it was the constant arguing or the messiness but something gave the house a negative feeling. My mom even said that she would get that same feeling walking into the house. It was odd.

When Bad Ethan Comes Alive

One day after school, my mom came to my house with Ethan and the minute he walked in the door it was like he switched into "bad Deets." He started crying and screaming that his shirt was wet and he wanted a new one. He had just started acting up when he got inside. My mom even said "Dang, what happened he was being so good until we got here." That's when it hit me! He can somehow sense the negative vibes in the house the same way my mother and I could. I thought it was strange but then my mind started to ramble on and things were just starting to click. The environmental surroundings have a lot to do with his behavior!

It applied even when we went to my great-grandmother's house. Every time we pulled up to her house he would release this horrifically loud scream. It was as if we were beating him. But really it was just that he could sense the negativity. Every time he went, we would all be on our toes because my great-grandmother is getting old and would get cranky and act out sometimes and every time Ethan was there she wanted to find him doing something bad and want to hit him. I'm not kidding. One time he plopped onto her bed and she immediately hit him dead in the face. Now, keep in mind she is almost 80 years old and apparently has a few serious conditions and she still managed to keep her posture and her balance and hit him hard enough to leave a mark. So I can understand why he didn't like going over.

As creepy as it is, he knew that it was not a place always filled with positive and good energy. He was smart and knew what was good and what was bad. I give him kudos for that. And don't think I let my great-granny get away with hitting him, I did explain that he does not understand. Now don't get me wrong, I love her deeply! She means a lot me and she's not always like this, I am just using this particular incident as an example.

Listen

Negativity can be sensed. It was just a little surprising that kids with autism could sense it. They have a knack for this sort of thing. So if your kid does not like a certain place, then that's a sign that maybe it's not such a good place. If there is one thing that I learned from this, it is that we should always listen to the kids and always follow our gut instincts.

TOXINS IN THE ENVIRONMENT

There are so many bacteria, viruses, and nasty toxins in the environment today, it is sick. All of these bad toxins like mold, smog, and cigarette smoke hurt us. Some help us loose focus and most lead to illnesses and conditions such as cancer, asthma, allergies, ear infections, bronchitis, and even a stroke.

If all these things can affect us in these ways, then you can only imagine how bad individuals with autism are affected. Most of them have major immune issues and if all these toxins, bacteria, and viruses keep hitting them, then it will eventually keep weakening their immune system.

Our immune system helps us fight infections and keeps us healthy. If we have a weak immune system, that means we will be more prone to catch an infection or possibly even worse. Many of these autistic kids get severe and constant fevers, ear infections, and some of them even get seizures. For those of us that have children that suffer from constant seizures, know that fevers and infections make them more prone to having a seizure. Therefore, this is just one of the many ways a weak immune system can be hurtful to those with autism.

How to Boost the Immune System

Sure, there are pills and meds that are advertised to boost an immune system but really we cannot trust all of them. Especially, since they all claim to be the best. It's like diet pills; can you really trust them all? Not all of them work because they all have different standards. One way to boost your immune system nice and easy is by reducing sugar intake.

Sugar weakens white blood cells and white blood cells help fight infections. If we have weak white blood cells then the chance of us getting an infection is pretty high.

According to a study done by the Loma Linda University shows that glucose[4], fructose[5], sucrose[6], and honey (as well as orange juice) can weaken the immune system's ability to get rid of the bacteria in our bodies. The study was published in the *Journal of Clinical Nutrition*. This study proves this that by reducing the sugar intake, it can help to boost the immune system.

Substitutes such as maple crystals can be used instead of sugar. You can purchase maple crystals in health food stores and markets or you can make them yourself.

[4] Sugar

[5] Fruit Sugar

[6] Table Sugar

Chapter 8:
Seizures

"His is not letting... his seizures stand in his way!"

- **Tina Fougere**, Mother of Nathan Fougere and Founder/President of CNAF

I am so glad that Ethan is one of the lucky ones that does not have seizures. I have heard of many cases where families suffer in fear because their children are constantly seizing. I even read a story of a woman who lost her son to a seizure after he went into cardiac arrest. It is a very sad but very important issue. I know Deets doesn't get them but I felt that this chapter is important to include in this book. I have asked around and found one woman who was willing to share her story. Her name is Carmen and she agreed to write a story but unfortunately she pulled out at the last minute because she was unable to. Her son's seizures are so severe and so constant that she has to have her eye on him at all times. Though she was unable to write a story I did find another woman that was able to. Her name is Tina and she is the President and Founder of the Canadian National Autism Foundation.

Here is Tina's story:

Nathan Fougere's ASD Diagnosis and Seizures
By Tina Fougere

We have twins Nathan and Tasha who are now 16 years old. The day that we noticed something was different with one of our twins was around the age of one.

When they were in the bathtub Nathan was not responding like Tasha was. We did noise tests beside his ears to see if he could hear us. We thought that it was an infection blocking his hearing. Sure enough, he did have one. But as the months and years went on, nothing seemed to have changed. Ear infection, after ear infection, medication after medication, it seemed that he had persistent infections.

For some reason that I cannot explain, I kept a daily diary of everything from the time I found out I was pregnant. Nathan did have words but was losing them around the age of one. I compared the two of them on a charting system using comparisons with speech, socialization, fine motor and gross motor skills.

The number of ear infections I documented at last count was as many as 85 plus from the age of one and three years old. I told my doctor "look something is wrong with my son" and explained everything I had documented. Of course even back then it is the same as what is said now, "He is just a boy and boys are behind in speech." I replied, "But look, the amount of ear infections is quite alarming to my husband and I. We see that he is not where his twin is in speech and interactions when they were approximately one and a half to two years old. Developmentally everything else Nathan did before Tasha. Crawling, rolling over, and walking a little before Tasha. He was even toilet trained at three." The doctor told me not to worry. In my anger and frustration because now Nathan is just over three years old I told him, "Look if I found out there was something wrong with Nathan and you did nothing to help I would have your ass in court faster than you could imagine." Well his mood changed and we went to an ear, nose, and throat specialist within a few days. He took one look at Nathan`s ears and had him in for tubes two days later. After the tubes were put in to drain his ears the doctor told us that Nathan's ears were a mess and he should have been looked after sooner. He was not impressed with our family doctor and said he was going to write a letter to the Medical Ethics Board about our family doctor.

Weeks after the tubes, we still did not really see too much of a change in Nathan's development specifically with his speech. He could hear us but something was not right, I could just felt it. I could not put my finger on it, but as a mom I knew.

I booked an appointment with our pediatrician and he asked us, after talking to me about both kids and checking them out, if anyone ever mentioned autism to us. I told him "No." He in turn booked us with a pediatric specialist in autism.

My husband and I went to see Dr. Rosenbaum with both of our kids who were now about three years and two months old. We were told that Nathan hkas Borderline Mild Pervasive Developmental Disorder (PDD). The doctor watched Nathan and Tasha play together and suggested this diagnosis. He asked us to come back in about four months for another assessment to see if there are any changes with his overall development with speech, fine motor, and gross motor skills

We went back home and said, "Okay, now we know what it is, let's start to help him." This is what we did. I looked for a lot but it was too much information. I just started tape recording my voice saying the alphabet and pointing to the letters and would play it back to him. I would video tape myself doing things and explaining things to him and then I would play to him so that he had

Saving Deets!

something visual and something concrete which I
knew was important. There was a lot more in
between of course that we did too.

Our next appointment came and the kids
were now almost three and a half years old and
were playing together but being loud on the floor.
The doctor said they, "we are sorry but they made a
mistake with Nathan`s diagnosis. Nathan does not
have Pervasive Developmental Disorder (PDD)." I
asked "But why did you say he did." He responded,
"Nathan is grasping everything at his age that he
should. He knows his colors and he puts them
together, he is interacting appropriately, but his
speech is behind. Nathan may be just a little behind
but I would like to see Nathan again in another
four months," which would make Nathan roughly
three years and nine months old. We were so lost. I
wondered, well then what was wrong for Nathan's
speech to be so far behind? We went home
devastated saying "Oh my God. What the hell
could be wrong?" How could a specialist have
made such a horrendous mistake in the first place?

I just kept working with Nathan the way I
did, his twin Tasha was also helping. We got the
whole family to do the same. I have three nieces
that were a very big help as well. They are nine
years older than Nathan and Tasha.

Our next appointment came. This time I
was prepared. I took a tape recorder and taped the
whole conversation. I told the doctor that I was
going to tape this appointment conversation
because we need to know what exactly our son has
so that we can help him NOW and that it is hard to
concentrate on everything being said with both kids
here. Dr. Rosenbaum was not impressed that I was
taping the conversation. He then proceeded to say
that yes they were right in the first place Nathan`s

diagnosis is Borderline Mild Pervasive Developmental Disorder (PDD). We left there thinking "Okay now Nathan has a diagnosis, now what?" We received some help from professionals like SLP (OT to show us how to work with him) but that is what we were already doing. It was a devastating time, but Nathan was making a lot of progress in our eyes. We saw no difference between Nathan and Tasha except he was being taught things at a younger age that what he was, and his speech was still behind by a lot. Understanding simple things was very hard for Nathan to comprehend. He had peripheral vision that he would constantly move his eyes back and forth while walking looking at the side of a table and the side of a truck from front to back constantly while looking sideways but not turning his head. Nathan would also bang his head on the floor and chew his clothes but these were all things that we could help redirect him from doing. Yes, it had been tough and a challenge but doable in our eyes. We were told Nathan would probably never go to school or talk. This was not acceptable to us or something that we were going to take lightly. We knew that Nathan would talk and he would go to school. They were just doctors going by the book they were not Nathan's parents and they did not know the determination we had to help our son.

At about the age of three and a half, Nathan started to stare into space. I told the pediatrician about this and he booked Nathan an appointment to have Electroencephalogram (EEG) done (which records the electrical activity of the brain through the wires that they paste on Nathan's head). My husband Duane, daughter Tasha, and myself went to help Nathan to stay calm as this test is confusing, the tabs being stuck to his head and all around scary for him to have done. Nathan did great being still and calm for the tests. He was wonderful and doing as he was told to try and stay calm and stay still. We were then told the tests showed nothing abnormal. I thought, "Maybe he is like the rest of us who sometimes like to just stare off into space. However, when there is a label it becomes a big deal, everything is brought back to the label. We also thought that he might have been having absence seizures. His home support worker, Christina, who is educated as well as trained in working with special needs kids, even noticed them when she came to take him out. He would stay still, stare straight ahead, and you could not get him out of it. Then he would come out of it himself, and say "Okay let's go" like nothing happened. This type of behavior with the staring off into space continued for a number of years, but never seemed to increase in intensity or duration.

At the age of twelve while Nathan was in the 7th grade, I was called to come to the school because something was wrong with Nathan. I went and he was in the nurse's room with The 8th grade teacher that I trusted and his Educational Assistant that he has had for six years now. He looked like he had fallen asleep and was waking up, but he was listless and incoherent. The two of them stated that that they think Nathan had a seizure. I took him home and called the doctor to book us in with a Neurologist. This took a few weeks. We went to have another EEG, that Dr. Meany from McMaster Hospital recommended, and there was again nothing. Dr. Meany concluded that it was not a seizure. We continue to see little stares into space and we were convinced they were indeed absence seizures that lasted for just seconds and he was fine. But we made everyone aware of them just in case the doctor was wrong.

Nothing else had been seen until the 8th grade. I was called by the secretary and told to immediately come to the school as they believed Nathan was having a seizure. My daughter, Tasha, also called me crying to come to the school but I was already at the school in the parking lot waiting for school to finish. They wheeled Nathan from class to the office so that the students would not be afraid and to give Nathan more privacy. The secretary as well as the principle called 911 two separate times but the ambulance was not coming. I asked the secretary to run out in front of the school and get my friend who is a fire fighter but was off duty to come in. He came into the school to help Nathan. My husband was there at that point with Tasha. The fire fighters were there as well as my friend who kept checking Nathan's vitals until the ambulance came.

When we got Nathan to the hospital, they did another EEG and a CAT scan, which gives a three dimensional picture of Nathan's brain and scull. Nathan did great so that he did not get sedation for the CAT scan as I just slowly explained to Nathan, "If you do this we can go right home, okay but you must stay very, very still like when mommy says freeze you have to freeze." I told him he was going into a donut machine. The doctors concluded that he had a seizure.

From that point on we kept a close eye on him and could most often pin point when and what time he would have a seizure. We fought putting Nathan on meds for five months as no one could promise me that Nathan would not have negative side effects from them as we know that things react differently with people on the spectrum. The seizures increased in the frequency, both in the number of seizures each month, and even each day. We then let the doctor know that we need to put Nathan back on meds and he suggested Topomax. Nathan was fourteen years old, in the 9th in High School at this point. Once on Topomax the seizures did not increase in frequency, but they also did not decrease. Within four months the seizure frequency increased, so we had the doctor give us permission to increase Nathan's dosage. We noticed after five months of being on Topomax that his behavior escalated to yelling, scratching his arms, biting his arm, daily migraines that lasted from morning until night every day, and as well as stomach aches. We went to see the neurologist to explain the situation of what Nathan was going through on the Topomax on and asked him if Nathan could be taken off since they were not helping; they, were in our eyes, hurting him more. The doctor suggested taking him off but also starting him onto another one at the same time. We decided that because the Topomax was not decreasing the number of seizures and the side effects he was experiencing, we would not put Nathan on any new medications for the time being. We weaned Nathan completely off of the Topomax.

After about five months of being totally off of the seizure medication, we noticed that Nathan indeed needed to be on some sort of seizure medication, but it would have to be a different kind. Nathan now is about fifteen years old. The doctor suggested that we put him on Topirmate. This we found to be better for Nathan. The only side effects that Nathan seems to have had and still does are his head/scalp is dry and he scratches it a lot. As well his arms are also very itchy.

Nathan continues to have quite a few seizures. For the first five months we could predict what day and what time he would have one. Now that we had to increase is medication dosage we can no longer predict when and how many he may have in a day. Nathan may have one seizure one day, and then the next day having five to nine of them. Then Nathan might go to having them once every week, to two times a month. Nathan's seizures are all Grande Mal seizures now.

The last seizure that Nathan had was just one seizure at night, and then another one the next day at supper time while he was eating. Out of the blue he fell backwards while eating and banged his head and was seizing while choking on his food. Tasha had to help me turn him over while I was trying to get the food out of his mouth. It was coming out of his nose and mouth as he was choking. Tasha was so upset by all of this since this is a lot for her to see and to go through with her twin brother with helping me with him when he is having a seizure. I was devastated; I thought that we were losing him. Thank goodness Tasha knows what to do, and will help as soon as something with her brother happens. Tasha has even told the school what they are to do when she knows Nathan is having a seizure. But thank goodness that is now not too much because his Educational Assistants and the Principle (who Nathan looks up to) knows exactly what to do and what not to do. They know not to call an ambulance for Nathan when he is having a seizure as I will be there in time to get him. If an ambulance is called and Nathan becomes aware of the fact the he is seizing, it only makes things worse. This can be very serious if this happens as it would be hard to get them back out of it without going to the hospital to make sure they do not keep continuing. I can say I trust the people who watch over Nathan at school which is a hard thing for me to do as trust comes hard for me with my kids because of the situation.

These last few years since Nathan started having Grande mal seizures it has been very hard for Tasha. This is her twin brother who has autism. They fight like typical teenagers but she is such strength when helping her brother through his seizures. When he comes out of them he wants to see her and have her sit with him.

Nathan does not remember what has happened during a seizure, but he does let us know before he has them at home. He tells us he is cold and wants a blanket and will lie down. Nathan also tells us "no ambulance, no hospital" as we have had an ambulance come many times to take him to the hospital because of his seizures. At school they know from what I have explained to watch out for such things as: when he goes very quiet, says he has a head ache, or has gray skin and goose bumps on his arms. He may also say call, "Mom!"

Nathan is a fighter we have witnessed him fight off seizures. We are all not sure how, but he has done this many times. It is a shame that life has to be restricted for him now that he is having seizures. With swimming we need another adult with me just in case. He needs twenty-four hour supervision. He cannot shower alone or be in the washroom on his own. Sad for his independence at sixteen and a half years old, but it is a must for safety. He has had two seizures in the washroom at home already. Doors have to remain open now and a monitor has to be in his room as he has had some seizures late at night and very early in the morning in bed.

To us as a family it is another direction in Nathan's life, a new adventure.

To end this with what we truly believe and for all to really take away from this story, our twins are our gifts from God. With all of the challenges that Nathan's autism and seizures have presented our family with, we treasure the talents that Nathan also has as well. He is a talented artist and he is very proficient on the computer. He is able to do things on the computer that we are not able to figure out! He can recite books word from word and lead us to the right place of where we are driving to even if he has not been there before. He has amazing and gifted photography skills that just leave us in awe. As well, Nathan has been admired for his photography talents by other photographers.

Every day is a new adventure for Nathan and our family, and he is not letting his autism or his seizures stand in his way!

Duane & Tina Fougere
Kids Nathan and Tasha, 16 ½ year old Twins
July 2009

Saving Deets!

Chapter 9:
Digestive Issues & Autism

"The answer for me lay in the slow but steady improvements we began to see."

-   **Kate Movius,** Mother of Aidan Movius and Advocate for Autism

I was doing interviews for my book searching for families that I knew or that would like to share their stories. I asked a friend of mine that I met through Autism Speaks if she would like to tell her story. She told me to go to a woman by the name of Kate Movius. Kate was also involved with Autism Speaks but since I was still so new at the time, I didn't know who she was. I looked her up on Facebook and sent her a message.

Weeks later, we set up a time and day for a phone interview. It was set up for Monday of the following week. Then, Monday passed. Then, Tuesday passed. No call. I thought that maybe she forgot. I sent her another Facebook message and no response. So then I decided to call her up. Keep in mind, I still had no idea where I was going to fit her story yet, then once we spoke on phone, it all became clear. She was at the hospital because her dear son, Aidan, was there for chronic intestinal difficulties. The next day, she broke down all the details to me and then it hit me. I completely forgot about this part! Ethan never had too many digestive issues before so it never really hit me to include a chapter about it. Though, my other brother EJ suffers from constant digestive problems but he is not autistic. It wasn't until I read *Healing and Preventing Autism* by Jenny McCarthy and Jerry Kartzinel, that I knew that it was common in autism. So I asked Kate if she would please share her story about her constant struggle with Aidan.

She agreed and here is her story:

Aidan's Journey

By Kate Movius

For the parent of a special needs child, trying to navigate the complicated world of possible treatments can become a full-time job unto itself. When my son was three years old and newly diagnosed with autism, my husband and I spent hours surfing the web every day, researching everything from swimming with dolphins to Applied Behavioral Analysis (or, "ABA"), a well-researched therapy used to help children learn to listen and follow directions. Like many parents, we settled on a kind of patchwork approach to treating Aidan's autism: ABA, Floortime, occupational and speech therapies. We also decided to try a gluten-free casein-free (GFCF) diet for Aidan, since, in addition to his autism, he had chronic diarrhea. We had heard from several other parents that removing gluten and casein (a protein found in almost all dairy products) had led to improvements in their children's gastrointestinal functioning, as well as breakthroughs in cognitive and social areas, such as speech and eye contact.

Since he was already a very skinny kid, we asked our Regional Center for a feeding specialist who could work with us to ensure Aidan was getting adequate calories and nutrition. Our pediatrician also supported our efforts, though was initially skeptical about claims that the GFCF diet could significantly improve the outcome for kids with autism. "As long as he's eating enough healthy foods, I don't see a problem with it," he said. Next, came the hard part: my son's diet consisted almost entirely of French toast, grilled cheese sandwiches, and chicken nuggets. WHAT WAS HE GOING TO EAT??

Fortunately for me, I had a friend who had already made this seemingly impossible lifestyle change. She had put her son on the diet several months earlier, and had seen great results. She came over to my house with three bags of groceries and showed me how to make gluten-free French toast with tapioca bread. She gave me a GFCF cookbook (written by another mom) which I was able to use somewhat successfully, in spite of the fact that I can cook just about as well as I can jog: haltingly, with lots of moaning and complaining. But the homemade gluten-free chicken nuggets? After serving Aidan a plateful of what looked and tasted like clods of concrete, I turned to the miracle of Whole Foods, where they sold frozen gluten-free "Dino Nuggets".

Yay! Leave it to Whole Foods to save the day. I don't mean to interrupt but Whole Foods is by far my favorite grocery store. They have everything there! It's like a Target with a grocery store and less clothes. The best part is: EVERYTHING'S ORGANIC! Love it! I used to hate going to the grocery store but Whole Foods changed that. Thanks Whole Foods!

Also, I feel Kate when she says that it is hard trying to make the transition to GFCF. It's tough. Ethan loved "Dino Nuggets" too and just about every other unhealthy processed meal.

Aidan adjusted to the change fairly easily –I was the one who struggled with the transition. I was tired all the time, it seemed; tired of driving him to and from therapies, tired of constantly monitoring his therapeutic progress, tired of the grief which would well up in me at the park, at birthday parties, or just sitting alone with him at home as I watched him struggle to engage with the world. I began to realize the extent to which I attached emotional comfort to food, both for myself and for Aidan. Couldn't he (and I) just have some ice cream after working so hard all day? Why did I have to isolate him even further by limiting his diet?

The answer for me lay in the slow but steady improvements we began to see in Aidan almost immediately after removing gluten and casein. We had decided not to tell any of his therapists that we were putting him on the diet – all the better to see if changes truly were taking place. His occupational therapist was the first to notice a difference: "He had the best eye contact I've ever seen," she reported with a smile on day three of the diet. His ABA therapists both reported that he was much more "present" and able to follow direction and had hardly cried during his therapy session (in those dark, early days, our now-happy boy would spend many hours each day in tears). But perhaps the most definitive improvements we saw were in his digestion. For the first time in over eighteen months, Aidan had a normal poop! We watched and waited to see if these changes were more than just a collection of happy coincidences. As the weeks went on, Aidan became a much more relaxed child. And it made sense: the better he felt physically, the more progress he was able to make cognitively and behaviorally.

Aidan is now eight years old. In spite of the continued challenges autism places in his path, he has made great progress in the areas of social connectedness, language, reading and self-regulation. But like many kids on the autism spectrum, his development does not follow a linear order: he will experience months of progress followed by periods of difficulty and occasional short-term regression. This spring, he had a terrible bout of the stomach flu followed by eight weeks of severe gastrointestinal distress. After many days of heart-breaking tears, several x-rays and a visit to a G.I. specialist, he has been put back on the path towards recovery. What remains clear is that – despite his behavioral progress and general physical heartiness – he remains extremely vulnerable to stomach distress. And when his gut ceases to work properly, his autism symptoms – mainly in the form of emotional distress and deregulation – eclipse his strengths.

Aidan's journey has been a long, brave, sometimes frustrating, but mostly beautiful one. Autism is perhaps the most complex of all disabilities because it does NOT follow one path; each child, and the strategies that work for him or her, are very different. We have found that maintaining Aidan's intestinal health is as important as his creating the best therapeutic team we can for him. Aidan deserves every possible chance for success in life and we are committed to helping him be as healthy as he can be as he works towards that end.

Saving Deets!

Chapter 10:
Tantrums &
Understanding

"It is alright to speak up and stand up."

- Zack Gonzalez

I t is very difficult to live in a society controlled by the media. We see so many families on television today and we want to live like they do: with the glitz and the glamour and the money and fame. We see autism as a punishment and keep questioning it.

It's hard to go out in public and try to ease my brother while he is throwing a tantrum. These people around us don't understand. They don't see that he is autistic and that he doesn't always know how to express himself the way we do. He's in his own little world. Many times I literally just want to punch that lady that is giving us that dirty look right in the nose but I just try to take a deep breath and remember that she doesn't know he has autism; she probably doesn't even know what autism is.

We always have to carry cards that say that "[Ethan] is not misbehaving, [he] has autism" (provided by TACA). Then once people get that shocked look on their face and apologize, I feel much better. I feel like, one, I helped spread awareness, and two, I was able show that person (or persons) that they need to be a little less ignorant, open their eyes a little more, and be a little more sympathetic. These are good feelings and I don't think that it's bad to consider these others around us as ignorant individuals because if they are so oblivious that they want to make mean faces and insulting remark, then yes, it *is* all right to speak up and stand up for Ethan.

Wait In Line!

I don't know how many times we've gotten those dirty looks for when Ethan is fussy in line. Anyone with an autistic child knows: They DO NOT DO LINES! It is just craziness. Deets cannot stand lines. He will either go running off somewhere or throw a tantrum. It's virtually impossible. The best method we use is to take turns.

Always bring a partner with you so that if you have to wait in line your partner can watch over the child meanwhile. My aunt is always tagging along with us so that we have one person in line, one watching Ethan, and one back up (just in case).

We also try to go places where lines are not a problem due to a disability, like Disneyland. One Christmas, we decided to go to Disneyland. It was so packed that day and the lines were super long. Luckily, one of the employees told us that we could get a card that enables us to move into the disabled line. We went to City Hall (at Disneyland) and got our little permit with the number of people in our party stamped on it and it was all a breeze from there. We didn't have to wait in any lines. We rode every ride there, some even twice. It was really worth it.

Obsessions

Ethan does a lot of crazy things. He has many of his obsessions with his shirts and with his trains. He gets so attached to these material items that it just makes me wonder. I don't fully understand why he does everything that he does but I try so hard. I try to look at the world as he does. It takes a lot of time to really understand him but it is something that helps so much.

Ethan goes through these phases where he gets really attached to his shirts. He started with his character shirts and then it changed to his soccer shirts, to his stripped collared shirts. He is always changing and as he changes I try to change with him. It is not easy, but the more I try, the easier it is to be more understanding.

Another obsession of his is that he loves cars! Whether it is a car from the movie *Cars* or it's a working car, he wants it. He claimed my mom's car as his own. Wherever that car went, he would have to go to or he would go ballistic. He would scream and cry, "My car is gone!" Another car he was attached to was my aunt's car. He called it his "Amber's Car." Whenever it was gone he would cry, "My Amber's Car is not here! Ahhh...Happen!!"

Every time something wasn't right or something happened that he didn't like or that shocked him, he would scream "Happen!!" It was his way off say "What happened?!" or "what the heck," (which he also learned to say).

Through all his little obsessions we tried to help him break them by getting him to try new things and wear new shirts. It was hard and he did throw little fits but little by little he learned that change was okay.

Routines

Sometimes they are so caught up in a daily routine that obsessions are much easier for them to develop. Like with Ethan, my mom allowed him to wear his shirt everyday so he got used to it. Then, once she saw that he was obsessed with it, she tried to break that routine and Ethan did not like that. He would scream and cry but my mom knew that it was the only way to break the habit. Same thing with school. Ethan was so used to the bus picking Monday through Friday, that when he would have a day off from school or he would go on vacation, he would flip! He did not like that.

Many times we just want to feed into to the kids and let them be, but really who are we helping if we do that? Sure, we will avoid the tantrums but that's not going to really solve anything. It's just going to feed into the child's inappropriate behavior.

TANTRUMS AT JUST THE RIGHT MOMENTS

So many times Ethan has thrown a tantrum at just the right moment; that moment that you would love for them to behave (like in public!). It drives me crazy sometimes. It is hard calming him down. First, I have to see what is wrong with him then I have to figure out how to help him through it. Sometimes we just have to distract him with something else. Other times we just have to ignore him because it may just be a way to get more attention.

Great Timing!

One day I was on the Autism Speaks website and I saw an ad for an upcoming documentary. It was an ad seeking families to feature in the documentary. I thought that this would be a great idea and a great way to share our story. I wrote into them and got a response right away. We filled out the application and went through the whole process.

It was about a week or two later and we received a phone call from a woman named Cynthia. She called to set up an appointment for them to come to my mom's house, meet the family, and do an interview. We set up the day and time. Everything was all ready to go.

It was finally the day for our interview and Jay had to work. So it was only going to be my mom, my brothers, and myself. So, we get to my moms house and immediately start getting ready and finishing up with the last minute cleaning. It was a bit of a mess because the house was under construction. There were extension cords and missing cabinets. It was not too bad but luckily they didn't mind it.

Ethan was outside playing with his cars in the dirt and decided to add water. Great! Now his car is all muddy and he is on the verge of throwing a fit. Then Sarah[7] arrives. She walks in and

---

[7] One of the women working on the documentary.

has to use the restroom. The bathroom has a lock but if you push the door it will open, regardless. So as she is in the bathroom, in runs Deets ready to wash his car because it is all muddy and wham! He pushed the door right open while Sarah was in the bathroom. I felt so bad for her! My mom ran right after him to get him and it was pretty crazy. So now he runs to the kitchen sink to wash it and then I think that now it's gonna be alright. Nope! Now he is crying because his car is soaked. So I give him a napkin to dry it but it was no use.

The car has mud in every little corner and in the wheels and it was a mess. Then Cynthia arrives and we start the interview. Ethan is still throwing his fit and now Cynthia has to speak over his screaming. I had to pull him aside and tell him that it is okay and I helped him clean it while the interview continued. Luckily, the ladies were very understanding and it was not too bad. Ethan was so good earlier that day and later that day but during the interview he was acting up. All I was thinking was "Great! Perfect timing Ethan!" It was the one time we would like him to behave and he was acting up. I could not blame him though. All I could do was help him get through it. I got him a fork to pick all the corners and he calmed down. He was fine for a while but then the interview was all over and we needed to take a picture. So now we had to get him and take a nice family photo. We did the best we could with him but the picture came up pretty funny with Ethan trying to run away. By the time they left he was much better. All it took was a little time to sit down with him and help him out.

Shut Up, and Listen, They Have Something to Say

Although, Ethan never spoke at a young age, he still had a lot to say. These tantrums that he was throwing were signs that he either wanted something or that something wasn't right. He didn't know how to express himself so he did it by crying and yelling. If he wanted attention, he would break something and get it. If he was hungry he wouldn't be quiet it about it, he would let the whole world know.

Saving Deets!

Though many times his little plans backfired. Like one time, we were babysitting my great-grandmother and he wanted to get us all crazy, so he made it look like he ate one of her pills. My mom freaked and went crazy! Instead of getting a kick out of watching her freak out, Ethan ended up in tears because he was scared because he had no idea what the heck was going on.

We need to make a stand for them. I love Deets dearly. He is my sibling just like Isaiah, Elijah (EJ), Joshua (Joshy), Shawn, and Breanne. If he needs me to speak for him, then I will be his voice. I needed to speak up on his behalf sometimes. It is not always a nice big piece of cake but it is something that I needed to learn how to do. I needed to dig really deep and find out WHY he was throwing this tantrum and WHY he wanted our attention. It is all about discovery. These children have a lot to say, we just need to figure out what it is!

Please note that some of the names in this chapter have been changed or modified for protection purposes

Chapter 11:
Expression

"Hey, as long as he loves it, I'm content."

- **Zack Gonzalez**

Ethan loves art! It's the best way to calm him down. He loves to write, paint, draw, color, and cut and paste. He uses art to calm down and express himself. If he sees you doing an art project then he immediately goes and jumps in.

One time we were making Thank You Cards with glitter and stamps. We were embossing the letters to make it look nice. Right away, Deets came right in and started to watch and observe what we were doing. Then, within five minutes he was stamping and embossing his own name. He loves art and loves to do little arts and crafts. It's like his little expression method.

We also use pictures of sad faces and happy faces and ask him "Deets are you sad?" or "Deets are you happy?" and he uses those pictures to express the way he feels. If he feels sad that he will say "sad," or "mad," or he will point to the picture. He isn't dumb; he knows how he feels and he understands what it means to feel happy, sad, or mad.

It took a while to see what methods work best for him and what helps him more. It didn't just happen overnight. We had to see what he reacts to and how he reacts to this compared to that. We tried a lot of different approaches and some worked, some worked really well, and some didn't catch his attention at all.

Art & Sports

Art is one of the main methods of expression that I've seen work really well. Our friend, Pam's, daughter loves to draw. She draws really well. She draws all her favorite characters. Pam has even come up with the idea to make them into index cards and now she sells them as a fundraiser method. Here is Pam's story on how her daughter got started:

Our Daughter Megan

By Pam Roumimper Eisenburg

Our daughter Megan was diagnosed with autism at twenty-six months old. She was non-verbal and had many behavioral issues that got her kicked out of many daycare programs because no one knew what to do with her.

After finally working with an agency and making some changes in her diet she was finally able to focus and really started making some progress. Megan really liked to color and paint. She started when she was two years old and made many cute pictures that helped her communicate with us. When she wanted something to drink, she would draw a picture of a glass and when she wanted to eat, she would draw a picture of an apple.

In 2006, I went to my first Autism Conference in Pasadena, California, with some other moms. I went because I wanted to see Temple Grandin speak. She was the first autistic woman that I knew of and her book, *Emergence,* was a book that I had read at least five times. It helped me understand a little bit of what Megan was feeling and what she was going through. After her speaking engagement, she was in the lobby meeting and speaking with parents and educators. I spoke with her and told her about my daughter having autism. She asked me what Megan perseverates and stims on the most. I told her that she likes to draw and color and that she does it and when she is happy, sad, angry, and frustrated. It was the only thing that calms her down. Temple looked at me and said, "You need to enroll her in art classes and this may help her develop her talent that you never knew existed." We enrolled her the next month.

Megan attended her first art class and she was there for about five months. She was five years old now and in a mainstream kindergarten class. She brought home the most beautiful drawings from art class! We thought everything was okay until we got a phone call from the owner of the art studio and she said that Megan was a disruption to the class and was very needy. They did not feel that this was the right class for her and asked that we remove her. We were so disappointed, upset, and confused! We believe in inclusion for all children and we thought other people did, too. We thought that we had found a perfect place for her to be around other children her own age, but it was not meant to be. She loved her art and we knew we needed to find a place that was more accepting.

When I read this, it made me a little upset. I just could not believe that they just straight out asked them to take Megan out of the class it was wrong. They could have been a little more considerate to the fact that Megan has autism. This just goes to show you how inconsiderate people can be. I'm pretty sure they could have worked around it but instead it looks like they took the easy way out by asking Megan to leave.

Finally when she started 1st grade we found a wonderful art class that had a smaller amount of kids and also some one-on-one, hands-on teaching. There were also two other children that had autism in the class. Megan has been there ever since. Now, the art classes that Megan takes is her outlet to decompress when the world starts to get too much for her. This is the one thing she can do to be alone, not be judged, and can express herself when people start to make too many demands for her to be like everyone else.

"Even the smallest person can change the course of the future."
- Galadriel (*The Lord of the Rings: Fellowship Of The Ring*)

Below I have include two of Megan's amazing drawings.

Giraffe by Megan Eisenburg

Another friend of ours, Gloria, has a son that loves art as well. He draws all his favorite cartoon and video game characters. He also loves to create pictures on the computer and animate them. He is very talented. Below are some of his computer creations:

Computer Creations by Aric Sule

In addition to drawing, Aric loves to swim and he swims very well. He has won metals at the Special Olympics' competitions. He is on an aquatics team. He loves it so much that one time he broke down crying because he wanted to swim and the Special Olympics didn't allow him to. Here is Gloria to tell you the full story:

Aric's Story

By Gloria Sule

Lots of things change, when you are told you child has autism. You're thrown into a world of worry but of all the things there is to worry about, sports weren't on the top of my list. At least it wasn't for me.

I guess I didn't realize how much our kids end up getting excluded. When the time came for Aric to start playing sports, I couldn't wait to get him on a team or on any team for that. Just somewhere where he can play with other children.

Then I saw the local parks where excepting applications, for the local little league teams. I was so excited. I couldn't wait to see my boy in his little baseball uniform. Thinking of how cute he would be. He'd be just like all the other kids his age. Well that never happened. Every park worker gave me the same story "Oh, I'm so sorry we are not capable of handling children with special needs children; we don't have qualified staff."

So, among all the other things that were going on and all the other places we were being rejected by, I couldn't even find my son a team. I felt so bad. And I would cry. I couldn't understand why they couldn't just let him play. Just let him hit the ball! Just let him try! Help me, help him make some friends. All the other kids had friends. I often asked myself "why?!"

One day I was especially sad and I started thinking there had to be a place where he would be accepted. There just had to be. And all of a sudden it came to me. I did it; I found the perfect team! It was the ultimate team! It was the Special Olympics of Southern California.

So when he turned seven and was able to participate I tried to find him a swim team. According to the coach Aric had to try out, so he did. Though he swam all the way across the pool I was told he wasn't good enough. The coach said that she would try to put him in some races but that didn't really make any sense to me "he wasn't good enough but she would put him in some races," okay? I knew there had to be something he would be able to do, I mean the boy could swim, awkwardly as he did, he could swim. So she finds him a race. It was an assisted swim (which means there would be someone behind him in case he needed them) but when the time came to race my son bolted across the pool and won his first gold medal in the Special Olympics! We were all so exited for him my son! He had a ginormous grin ear to ear. I was the proudest mom in the whole world.

Then the coach said he qualified for summer games in Long Beach, CA. She said it was a big deal and she would get him in an assisted swim again but that there were a lot of rules for summer games. One, we would not be able to go in certain areas with him and that alone sounded bad to me because I knew my son would need me. I knew no matter how much I explained to them how to take care of him they would not be able to or willing to do it I knew things would get bad oh and they did.

It was the first day of summer games 2006 and my son was seven. The pool area was closed off to families and there were so many races going on. I told his coach to please not leave him alone. I told her lots of things, one was to please make sure he didn't hurt himself (since my son was self-injurious) and to make sure he didn't throw himself in the pool because if no one was looking after him he would. I told her he was quick and I told her I was worried. I think I was more like begging her at one point because I felt she didn't care and wasn't listening. All I thought was "please be careful with my son" but I knew they wouldn't. She had a couple of assistants that I had also explained things to and they were all like "yeah, yeah, don't worry." Me? Not worry? Ha! That would be the day. In my heart I knew what was coming but I left

I went to the designated area and waited. I waited and then my cell phone rang. It was the coach. Apparently, Aric threw himself in the pool while they were racing and the officials decided to kick him out of the pool area and scratch him off the rest of his races! My heart sank when I met up with the coach face to face. I literally had to drag my son away from the area while for the first time he shouted "Nooo! Mom no! I want my friends! I want my friends!" For me, hearing him say those words for the first time was amazing but sad at the same time because I could do nothing about it. I couldn't just let him back in. My sister took him from me as I was telling the couch how unfair it was to not let him continue to participate, especially, since it was their fault for not watching him properly. Everyone was staring since my son was still shouting "Stop!" They just all looked at us. "Stop staring!" I thought. If anyone understood what I went through it was these people but it didn't feel that way.

That day I can't even put into words how I felt. I just can't so I told the coach she better get back in there and tell them we were not leaving until he finishes his races or did she want me to go in there and tell them!! That and how it wasn't my sons fault he wasn't being watched the coach went to tell the officials and they told her to tell me he could finish his races and he did. He didn't do very well but at least he participated and that's all I've ever wanted. When I got home I got a call from the coach and she said she was just calling to let me know that the races scheduled for the next day where canceled. "That's fine" I said. I didn't hear from her again until I decided to try again and I got a hold of the Southern California Special Olympics and they directed me to the same coach. Okay, we all know that didn't work out they said they had nothing else he would be able to do I decided not to think about it again until I moved to another city. I thought maybe they had more options in new area. I was right. I was directed to Norwalk, where my son joined the track team and softball. The coaches have been great. They are everything I've always wanted; everything my son and others deserve. The love caring and understanding is there. The coaches have gone above and beyond my expectations. The truth is that they made my dreams come true

My son has gotten a lot better since he's gotten older but he still has his moments. The melt downs are still there at times and they're totally fine with it. They don't see anything but what I see: a beautiful boy who just wants his friends; who just wants to play!

Wow, my experience with the psecial Olympics has been interesting. It's been very bad, yet, very good. Thank god the good always outweighs the bad.

My son got back in the game and in early 2009 he made it back to the Long Beach summer games. He has won so many gold medals and made so many friends. 2009 was an amazing year thanks to the

Southern California Southeast Los Angeles staff for team Norwalk. Go team!

I started my story with all of the things there are to worry about. Sports weren't on top of my list. When I read this to my husband he said it was on the top of his list. I had no idea until now!

Thank You,

Aric's Mommy, Gloria Sule

Aric and Mommy

Ethan also loves to play sports. He plays soccer and baseball. He is obviously not the MVP but he loves to play and hey, as long he loves it, I'm content.

He would always run out on the field when EJ was playing soccer and would try to go out and run with the other kids during the games. My mom was the coach, so she didn't have a problem with it but sometimes the others coaches would get a little upset, but who cares!

After soccer season, my mom finally put Deets in baseball. She was, again, the coach. Ethan liked to play and he knew when his and EJ's practices were and he would grab his uniform and start cheering, "Let's go Yankees! Let's Go!" At the time, he was on the Yankees team in t-ball and EJ was on the Giants team in 5 Pitch. So anytime there was a game or practice, Deets would have to get geared up. He also enjoyed going to Dodger games. He would cheer and scream. He would have a blast!

Film Making

Another thing that can be used as a form of expression is film making. Many individuals on the spectrum have at least one talent that they do exceedingly well in. For this next extraordinary young man, it is film making. He is the creator of the film *Normal People Scare Me*.

I first met his mother at the 2008 Walk Now for Autism and as I was seeking vendors for my Play Now for Autism event, I came across her once again. Her name is Keri Bowers and she, too, is an independent film maker.

After visiting the Autism Talk Radio website and listening to her interview months later, I decided to give her another call. I asked her if she would like to write a story for my book and she said yes.

Here is the amazing Keri Bowers to tell the story of how her son first got started and the success that came from it:

Normal People Scare Me

By Keri Bowers

nor·mal (nŌr′məl), **adj.** 1: perpendicular ; *especially* : perpendicular to a tangent at a point of tangency 2 a: according with, constituting, or not deviating from a norm, rule, or principle b: conforming to a type, standard, or regular pattern 3: occurring naturally <*normal* immunity> 4 a: of, relating to, or characterized by average intelligence or development b: free from mental disorder (Merriam-Webster Online Dictionary).

"What is 'normal' anyway?" Taylor asks the audience. At 6'10" with long blonde curls, Taylor stands tall and erect flashing a big smile as he muses. Taylor knows that so-called normal is a word used to describe the indescribable. "I don't think there is such a thing as normal because to me, everybody is strange; people in general are definitely not so normal in my eyes."

Why then did you call your film "Normal People Scare Me?" people ask. He laughs. "I saw it on a t-shirt and it just fit."

Today at 20 years old, Taylor does not define himself by the label of autism which was given him at the age of 6. Though he has worked hard all his life to overcome the challenges and idiosyncrasies of the disorder, he knows he is unusual if not entirely quirky. For this, he makes no apologies or excuses. "I just am what I am" he says. "It is the rest of the world that has the problem with people like me who don't fit into the world's idea of "normal."

Taylor's love of film had always been central to his life. Film was – and still is – his perseveration; his passion. When he was five years old with delayed language, Taylor found it hard to relate to the daily rigors of the world. It was difficult for him to describe his needs and wants, and to share his inner-world. And so it was his love of film, actors, directors, fantasy, and comedy that Taylor used to connect to the outer world. He could name all the actors, directors and other players in the various films in the Calendar section of the *Los Angeles Sunday Times*. He would let you know which films were currently screening, and which were soon-to-be released. He could name all the films his favorite actors appeared in. Through film Taylor connected to reality and to fantasy. In so many ways this is still true.

Taylor was 14 when he conceived the idea to make a film. Just before Christmastime, 2003, he asked me how he might earn money to pay for the holiday gifts we gave to families less fortunate than ourselves. We had traditionally adopted a couple of mothers and their children from a battered women's shelter in our community. Each year, I used this community service as an opportunity to teach Taylor and his brother Jace social and life skills. Each year the boys took on more and more responsibility toward the effort of gift giving.

In the beginning I dragged them along to the store and had them help select and wrap the gifts. "What kind of gift would a girl of eight like?" Taylor would always do his best to decide, sometimes choosing an inappropriate boys toy. As the years went by, the boys took on more and more responsibility to budget, make cards, and deliver the gifts in person.

Taylor enjoyed this yearly ritual. I believe he intuitively understood that others needed things (toys, books, blankets and other essentials) he took for granted in his world. For a boy in his "own world" he seemed to connect to our community service project in a meaningful way, and he learned much about sacrifice and giving to others in need.

"Mom, this year I want to pay for the gifts myself." Taylor announced. "How can I earn some money?" I suggested he clean the swimming pool. "Naaaagh!" he replied. "I want to make videos and sell them!"

"You can't make a film honey! People go to school for that." On and on I went, telling him every reason I could think of why he could *not* make a film. And then I caught myself in mid-sentence. As I searched his face, a vision crossed my mind. "Yea, and *they* told me you might never walk or talk, but we sure did show them didn't we?" The thought took my breath away.

"Taylor, everything I just said to you is a lie. You *can* make a film. I don't know how we will do it, but if you want to make a film, then I will help you." His eyes lit up. "You just need to know what you want to say. What would you like to make a film about?"

"I dunno." He replied.

"Well, I understand people should do what they know best. What about autism?" And that was it. We never looked back – just forward.

The world has a funny way of rising to the occasion of an essential dream. Once we put a thought or energy out into the universe, answers often appear in the strangest ways.

Through a series of events, One week later, Joey Travolta appeared in our lives. According to the article in our local paper, Joey was sponsoring a student film festival for his daughter's senior year of high school. The article also mentioned he had been a special education teacher in New Jersey back in the 70's. "How bazaar and perfect is that?" I thought.

At the time, in addition to directing and producing independent films, Joey was teaching acting classes to kids in the San Fernando Valley area of Los Angeles. I knew his classes would be a great opportunity for kids with autism who were students in the social skills groups I facilitated with my business partner, Alisa. We agreed that if we could get Joey to include *our* kids with typical peers everyone would benefit. We set up a meeting with the intention of encouraging Joey to see our vision of including kids with special needs in his classes – and hopefully to enroll him in helping Taylor to make a film.

To Joey's credit, his heart is big as it is open. Such light and passion is a wonderful quality in others. His receptivity to inclusion in his classes and our film project was enthusiastic - even more so than we might have imagined. To our utter delight, one month after that first meeting several kids from our social skills groups were successfully enrolled in his acting classes. Shortly thereafter, Joey began to mentor Taylor to make the original 10 minute student film, *Normal People Scare Me* in which Taylor interviewed five young people on the autism spectrum.

Some six months later, when the student film, *Normal People Scare Me* was screened at Chaminade High School in West Hills, California, we were surprised at the reception it received. Gleaning a couple of awards, including best in show, the short documentary also received reviews in local newspapers and Taylor received The Bubiel Aiken "Youth Champion of Change" award for his work in advocacy and education.

Before we knew it people from all over the world were contacting us to purchase copies of the short film which led to our making a feature-length version of the film.

The 90 minute feature film, *Normal People Scare Me*, would take one year to complete. Often we had to drag Taylor to the finish line – as it was not easy to have a young man with autism interview others with autism. Yet in the end we reached our goal of exploring autism from a vast vs. singular perspective. The film features first-person perspectives of life and living with autism by sixty-five individuals - children and adults – with different levels of abilities. As the interviewer, Taylor offers a quirky and refreshing interview style as he asked questions including: *"Do you like being autistic?"; "What do you want to be when you grow up?"; Have you been teased?, and "Do Normal People Scare You?" The result is a* powerful, poignant insight to the joys and sorrows behind the faces and mysteries of autism.

Today, Taylor has traveled all over the world to share his film and his work in Micro Enterprise (customized employment options) in which he worked closely with a business coach to help him with his own speaking tour – without Mom. Though he is still working on becoming more independent, today he stands on stages to ovations, and on a good day, to rave reviews. He currently attends community college – but not without many struggles and challenges. Despite any and all setbacks Taylor experiences as a young adult, he is always resilient and optimistic about his future.

I sometimes say of my son, "Taylor is neither of the heavens nor of the earth. He is somewhere in the clouds." And there in the middle is where he is happy to be. As for his new plan of action, Taylor is currently studying Japanese. One day he wants to move to Japan to make films. And you know, at his height, with his good looks, keen sensitivity, smarts, and determination while it might take him longer than some, he will likely make it in whatever he decides to do in his life.

"Mom," Taylor says, "We sure did and will show them!"

Keri Bowers is a parent, advocate, filmmaker and workshop leader. Her film projects with sons Taylor and Jace include *Normal People Scare Me, The Sandwich Kid,* and *ARTS.* Her workbook "Mapping Transitions to Your Child's Future" is a popular topic at workshops and symposiums around the world. Taylor continues to travel both with – and without mom. He currently works with support staff toward the goal of business development and independent living. www.normalfilms.com

Zack Gonzalez

Saving Deets!

Chapter 12:
Methods to Recovery

"Recovery IS possible."

There are many recovery methods out there and many that I have heard from other families that work really well. Such as the Special Carbohydrate Diet (SCD), Low Oxalate Diet, eating only organic foods, B12 Shots, and many other biomedical interventions, diets, and therapies. The ones contained in this chapter are only the ones that we have tried and that have worked for us. Keep in mind that they are not guaranteed to work for everyone but they have worked for many. They are specially designed to help the child's specific needs. Also, please keep in mind that I am not a specialist. This information is based on research and personal experience. Before starting any diet, you should always consult with a health professional first.

THE GLUTEN-FREE, CASEIN-FREE (GFCF) DIET

What ever we put into our body affects our brain. Diet is a big part of good brainpower. No matter what we do, we need food and water to function. When we eat badly it affects our body in a negative way. Many people do not see how a healthy diet can affect an autistic child's brain. When they eat healthier, it makes it easier for them to focus and function; when they eat badly it makes it hard for them to concentrate and work.

There are so many toxins in our food now days. There are too many pesticides and unhealthy preservatives in our food. Cows are being injected with estrogens and there are over seventy pesticides that go onto our fruit and vegetables. There are artificial hormones that are being injected into chickens and cows. All of this is not safe for our bodies. If we continue to give these children these bad foods then how are they supposed to function properly?

Many people see this diet as a cure to autism, but really it's not a cure. I don't see it as a cure, but I do see it as a method to help my brother overcome many of his symptoms. This meal plan is specially designed to remove the gluten[8] and casein[9] from their daily routine and help them recover much better.

After we heard about the GFCF diet and how it was such a huge help for many other families we decided to get Ethan started on it. We all came to an agreement that we were going to help him out by changing the way he ate. We were going to give him a whole new diet filled with GFCF meals.

My mom went and got him tested and we found out what foods he was allergic to and which ones were affecting him and in what way. Then, we started to begin the diet. We bought the food that's needed and broke down the meal plans to every member of our immediate family. Everything was all set to go and we got him started right away.

Do the Diet Even If Everyone is Against It

At first, it seemed like we were all the same page but little did we know, there were some of us that were not too happy about his change in diet. My grandparents gave off this odd vibe once we first started Deets on the GFCF. It was obvious that they were not fully up to helping with the diet plan. My grandmother, the way I see it, did not take too well the actual word "diet." I think she saw it as taking away from him more than it was helping him. My grandparents many times were against the diet and went head-to-

---

[8] A special type of protein found in most grains
(http://www.gfcfdoneeasy.com/index.php?option=com_content&view=article&id=52&Itemid=55.)

[9] A protein found in milk and independently used as a binding agent
(http://www.gfcfdoneeasy.com/index.php?option=com_content&view=article&id=52&Itemid=55).

head with my mother. It was not easy trying to help Ethan out when we had part of the family against the plan. They said that they did not see it working and that there was not much progress being made. Of course not, they were letting him get away with eating things he should not have been eating. They were not at strict with him as they should have been.

I could tell that my uncle, too, was against the diet. No matter how many times they said they would support it, I knew they didn't. I saw when they would act like they did not see him eating the jar of frosting and that pack of candy or pretend like they did not know what he was and was not supposed to eat, when the whole breakdown was given to them time and time again.

It is very difficult to do something and have so many people that are around Ethan go against what you are doing. Many times I tried to defend my mom and help her out when it was like they were attacking her but I could tell that they never really took me seriously. I was just seen as a kid helping his mom. I felt underestimated and at times when they would not even pay attention, it felt a little demeaning. I actually had an opinion and the way my opinions would go in one ear and out the other was hurtful, especially when I knew that I did more research than they did.

Though not all of them were against it. My aunt, Amber, was very supportive. She was very helpful and always made sure that he was not eating something that was not good for him. She was very active in Deets' life and is always after him. I respect her much more because I see how much work she puts into him. She is like his second mother.

If They Won't Take It, Make Them

Another person that was not fully up for the diet was Ethan. He LOVED his junk food and his sugary syrupy juices. What kid would want to give that up?

He was attached to his bad eating habits but it was not a matter of liking or not liking, it was a matter of healing. If we wanted him to start to recover then we really need to make it work. It was tough trying to get him to eat healthier; especially when all my grandparents had at their house was a lot of junk food.

He was like an addict addicted to drugs. When these children eat these substances they get hooked. It is like these foods are their opiates; they must have them. They will fight, bite, scream, and refuse but it is all up to us and whether we really want to help them.

Our first attempt at the diet made a lot of progress but without the full support of the rest of the immediate family, no drastic changes were made. He did work much better when he ate better, though. Before he would just run off at the stores and at the parks and after the diet, he did much better with staying with the family. He also started to write a lot more. He would spell all the names of his favorite characters from *Thomas and Friends* correctly. He also started talking much more and was learning how to express himself in a much healthier manner.

This diet did help him out and I know for a fact that once we get him started again and really make no exceptions, then it will be a key in to recovery. Now, the diet does not work for every child but it does work for the majority of those that try it. If you are going to put your child on this diet, you must make sure that you have them on 100 percent because that's the only was you are going to see recovery and improvements. Please be very careful on this diet and do not go to extremes. I do recommend doing a detox before starting the diet. To read more about the GFCF diet, there is a list of resources located at the end of this book. You can also find a few of our favorite recipes from our friend Nicci's website: (gfcfdoneeasy.com). There you'll find tasty GFCF recipes.

Next Attempt at the Diet

I am glad to say that we did end up getting much stricter with the diet and Ethan has been doing much, much better. He is reading and talking more. Now, we plan on doing a metal detox and hope for a full recovery.

AROMATHERAPY

After our first attempt with the GFCF diet, my mother got my brother started on aromatherapy. Every night before bed she would pull out a new scent and help him get all his senses in order. For example, one night she would pull out the orange scent and an orange and have him smell it, then touch and feel the actual orange and get him to see that what he was smelling, feeling, and seeing was an orange.

She used many other scents and objects with him and little by little he started to get the hang of it. Though he had his nights where her just wanted to eat the orange instead of actually doing the therapy that night. After a while of trying this new therapy Ethan started to read and speak better. He also started to write a lot more.

My grandpa bought him a chalkboard for him to write on and draw on. At first, we all thought it was dumb and useless because it was just a chalkboard and Deets would soon lose interest in it like all his other toys. We were a little upset with him for buying it because it took up a lot of room but little did we know Ethan would love it. This chalkboard is where he would write out all his words and draw matching pictures.

After doing the aromatherapy Ethan started to show great progress. He went to his chalkboard and drew cars and trains. One of my personal favorites is his "balloon car." He drew a car with a balloon on top of it and called it his "balloon car." He even wrote balloon car on top of it. He is always coming up with these funny little drawings.

This was one of methods we used that really did help. My mom found out about it from MAAP Services. You can go to www.maapservices.org to read more about the aromatherapy.

VITAMINS AND SUPPLEMENTS

Most doctors say that vitamins are no help. They say that they do not do anything for us and that they can be a waste of money. That is not necessarily true. Vitamins and supplements do work! We use them and they always help us a lot better than these drugs that the doctors and pharmacies give us. All of the crap that is given by the pharmacies and prescribed by the doctors is a bunch of drugs. They do not make money off of supplements so it makes sense that since they make more money prescribing some medication (that you cannot even pronounce), then they will give you those meds over vitamins any day. It's all about money!

My mother is always after my brothers about taking their vitamins and her, too. She is constantly drinking that Emergen-C to get her daily dose of Vitamin-C and she is hardly ever sick. Ethan takes plenty of helpful vitamins because they help him. There are vitamins out there that are designed for almost everything. From healthy brain function, to helping to keep a healthy immune system, to ones that help keep your skin and hair healthy. You can pretty much find a vitamin or supplement for virtually everything.

Now, I am no physician but I know by experience and by knowledge that vitamins and supplements *do* work. They work for me, they work for my family, and most importantly they work for Ethan.

To help you out I have included some tips from a professional company and a chart on supplements.

Kirkman Idea's On How To Easily Take Nutritional Supplements

- Mix in orange juice

- Mix in lemonade

- Mix in red grape juice

- Mix in pear juice

- Mix in baby food prepared juices

- Mix in Juicy Juice®

- Mix in V-8 Splash®

- Use yogurt

- Use pudding

- Use fruit sorbets

- Try Cocoa

- Try Hershey® syrup

- Try peanut butter, cashew butter or almond butter

- Make a fruit "smoothy" in a blender

- Make a protein drink (rice or soy) in a blender

- Use honey or jelly as a vehicle to mix products in

- Make Popsicle's which include the vitamins (especially good for the Super Nu-Thera® powders and liquids)

- Put doses of the supplements in "rice crispy treats"

- Sprinkle non-heat sensitive products on a pancake before flipping it over

- Put in ketchup and let the kids drag their french fries through it

- Put the products in scrambled eggs (after they're cooked)

- Put products in spaghetti sauce (after it's been cooked)

- Hide products (especially liquids) in "box drinks"

- If you use Coromega®, add other supplements to it

- Calcium, magnesium and Flax (EFA Plus) can be used in cooking and baking

- Baby foods work great in hiding supplements (the jr. ones even have some texture to them)

Obtained from:

http://www.kirkmanlabs.com/TakingSupplements.aspx

Another awesome alternative is the revitaPOP. RevitaPOPs are MB12 lollipops that give you your does of B12. They are an excellent substitute for B12 shots. We use them for Ethan and I have tried them, and I must say, they are amazing. They work really well and they are completely organic and all GFCF. You can purchase them on revtitapop.com or you can find a distributor. We are distributors and we sell them off of Jay's catering website. His website is bodyandsoulorganicfood.com.

Turn the page for a helpful supplement chart.

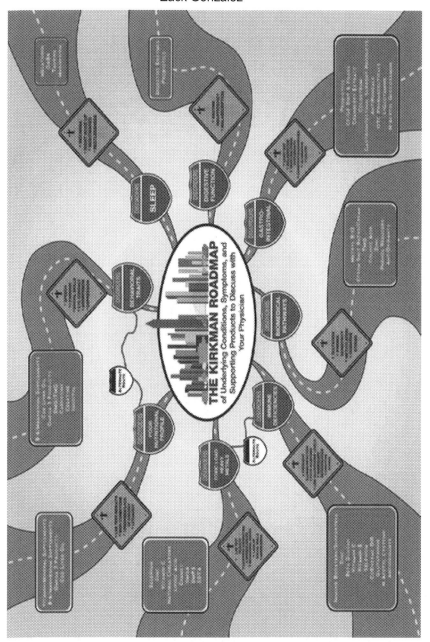

Chart obtained from: Kirkman's Biomedical and Dietary Intervention Beginner's Guide. www.kirmanlabs.com

FLASH CARDS

Another good technique is to use flash cards. My mom got Ethan a pack of flash card with pictures and words and they helped him read better. Eventually instead of just using the pictures to tell what the word meant, he would pronounce and read the word!

He makes me so proud. Flash card with numbers, pictures, words, and colors are very helpful. You can get them pretty much anywhere. They are easy to find, and easy to use. It is probably one of the best things we have used to help Deets read.

MUSIC THERAPY

One time, my mom got a pair of Dodger tickets from her friend Tina for a game that night. There were only two tickets and if she went she could only take one kid. So, since EJ loved Dodger games, either I went with him or she did. I agreed to go over to her house to watch Ethan and let her go with EJ. They went and hoped that if they went early enough that they could go and meet with Jay and the Box Club[10], where he worked. They ended up meeting some other guys and got two free field level tickets. So, they ended up staying for the whole game and planned on taking Jay home after work but he ended up finding another ride.

Late that night my mom and EJ came home. My mom wanted me to wait for Jay to get home and let him take me home since Deets was already asleep and she didn't want to take him out. So I waited and I waited and I waited some more. It was late and after watching another hilarious late night talk show, *Chelsea Lately*, I called it quits and fell asleep on the couch. Jay got home really late that night.

The next morning, my mom planned on having breakfast with a friend of hers but she also had a meeting with a mommy-group that she meets with regularly. So since I was with her that

---

[10] Restaurant at Dodger Stadium.

morning, I went with her. We met Gloria (remember her from the chapter on expression) and went to the meeting.

At the meeting, we learned about a new therapy: Music Therapy. Andy, the program director, told us all about it. It was fascinating! He talked about how you need to get the children involved in the music and experiment with instruments. He said that it was a way of letting the child be in control of his or her own environment. It helps to improve the child's attention span and explore all of their senses. He went on about how he does it and he showed us some videos of some of the children he had worked with. The improvements I saw were amazing! There was one child that shook Andy's hand and it was the first time he ever shook a persons hand and said hello for the first time. It was so awesome! To learn more about music therapy please visit:

www.memory-key.com/Language/music.htm

or

www.biopsychology.com/index.php?descType=always&id=6&type=keyword&page=0])

CHIROPRACTOR

By Nancy Quesada

Ethan also visits a chiropractor. When I first went to visit the chiropractor, Dr. Mike, Ethan was all over the place. He had a really weak upper body. Dt. Mike told me to keep bringing him in because he wanted to help Ethan built more upper body strength and hand grip. He was right. Ethan started climbing, hanging, and cutting with scissors.

His OT called me two months after treatment and asked if I was practicing cutting with Ethan because his gross motor grasp was stronger and just a month ago he had the grip of a one year old, now suddenly he was cutting like a five year old. I told her I just started taking him to the chiro.

Saving Deets!

Ethan loves Dr. Mike! He lies on the table, greets him, and is now much more coordinated.

Dr. Mike's Info:

Dr. Mike DeNapoli, DC

960 East Green St #302

Pasadena, CA 91106

Phone: 626-564-1605

Chapter 13:
Stand Up!

"We have spent the last 40 years thinking silence equals a lack of intelligence. Silence allows you time to listen. Listening offers unparalleled growth."

- **Eva Woodsmall,** Mother of an Autistic Child and Advocate for Autism

I t is hard to get people to listen and even harder to get them to care. When it's us against the pharmaceutical companies, who do you think people are going to listen to? Lets face it, unless enough of us stand up and speak up, nobody is going to listen. Not to us and not our children.

WE NEED TO FIGHT FOR OUR RIGHT TO BE HEARD

If people won't listen to us then we need to make them. If the world will not listen to what we have to say, then we need to make them! If your neighbor won't listen, you need to make them. If your mother won't listen, you need to make her listen. We need to make our claims vocal! We need to rejoice our wonderful kids! They are special and they deserve to be shown off! Why should we sit back and let people in a high position silence us. If I have something to say then, damn it, I will very well say it and say it loud! I think the vaccines have a lot to do with autism, and I'm not afraid to say it. I have plenty of opinions and the ones that matter to me, I will say and I will say them loud and clear, even if my voice shakes.

Don't Let Doctors Silence You

Many times our doctors and physicians tell us that there is no link to vaccines and autism. They think they know everything. When we families are at home seeing that there is some kind of effect on these children after they get a vaccine and we try to speak up about it, they shut us down. The muzzle us, those SOB's. Not anymore! I am proud to say that not all the vaccines are very healthy and that they are not all safe.

Why should I let a doctor tell me that my brother has autism because of one little gene? I think it's dumb and not fully correct. Hypothetically speaking, let's say it was genetics. Now my cousin is allergic to strawberries and this could be genetic, but if he never eats strawberries he is perfectly fine. Is it not possible that if my brother was never exposed to those vaccines that he would be perfectly fine as well. Of course!

I strongly believe in my heart that it was not genetics that brought Ethan to being autistic. There are so many other families out there shouting that the vaccines are hurting the children but we still are not being listened to. We ALL need to stand up and be very vocal about our opinions and then we will be heard. If not then we might as well just sit there miserably.

Another thing is that when we heal our children and recover them, the doctors say that they must have been misdiagnosed. Now that is a bunch of bull. How can you say that the child is and then isn't autistic. It was misdiagnosed? Are your joking? I don't think so. Is it not possible that a simple diet could help them out? They say that it is not possible to heal a child with diet and supplements or with certain therapies. The physicians, like I said, think they know everything. Just because they don't believe in the diet doesn't mean it doesn't work. Can I get an Amen?

Don't let your doctor silence you, if you believe something, say it. If you suspect something, ask it. If you don't agree with something, question it. If we let these doctors, and other officials for that matter, continue to speak over us then we will never be heard. They are the loud music playing in the background when we are speaking and all we have to do is all speak up louder and lower that music!

NEVER FORGET WHY

My mother and I were buzzing and booking ourselves for all these events. From bowling events to benefit concerts to picnics and meetings. We had our schedules booked! We were so busy trying to raise more money and going to all these other events for autism, we almost forgot why were doing it.

Ethan! He is the reason we were doing all these events. He is the "why." I didn't even realize it until I was at my mom's house in the living room, waiting as she was getting ready in her bedroom, and my step-father, Jay, and I were talking about getting his catering business started and my acting career going.

My mother walked into the room and mentioned that they were looking for a videographer for the upcoming Walk Now for Autism 2009 (now know as the Walk Now for Autism Speaks). She said that he would be perfect because he has such an open personality and he is loud and outgoing. Then he turned to her and said, "I would love to but what about Deets?" We looked at each other. "Who's going to spend time with him?" he continued, "It's his day and here you guys are booking yourselves for all this shit and you're forgetting why you are doing it." That's when I realized that I was starting to over-book myself and that I was volunteering too much.

We were doing it for Deets but really we were forgetting that volunteering at and attending all these events was taking away our time with him.

"Don't get me wrong, it's good what you guys are doing but just don't forget it's Deets' Day." I really started to think back and saw that I was doing all these events for him but I was not spending too much time with him at the events. I was too busy volunteering and running off doing something while he was either with Amber or Jay.

For once I actually felt pretty damn guilty for doing so much. Jay really made me think about it and I knew that I was starting to forget Ethan. I felt really bad and for a long time I didn't want to admit it. That's one thing that I like and hate about Jay: he is very blunt. He always speaks his mind. He is the one that passes out the reality checks and keeps everyone in line. He is the one who brings us down when our heads get too filled with air. I admire him for that, though it irritates me at times.

Please always remember that if you are going to volunteer and attend a bunch of events that you still make time for your children because they are the reason you are out there doing it.

Chapter 14:
Making A Difference

"It was truly a success after all!"

- **Zack Gonzalez**

N ow, I can't just go out and tell you to make a difference; I have to be a living example. So, here is the story of Play Now and how it all came about:

It was November, I had just gotten back from New Mexico, after visiting some family, and I was sitting with my mother at the doctors' office. It's actually a pretty funny, yet, gross story. On the train ride back from New Mexico I got a bacterial rash that broke out on my forehead and spread to the rest of my body (gross right). So my mom took me to go get it checked out. We were sitting in the waiting room watching a sporting event for children with special needs. Then we started talking about the lack of involvement in our community and about how we should bring awareness.

We came up with the idea to create our own baseball event for the local families affected by autism. We started tossing ideas back and forth and decided to make it a baseball game for kids with autism. Then, a male nurse walks out and calls "Gonzalez..." I looked up and walked through the pale walls into the office.

After the appointment, we walked out and headed home. In the car, we again, exchanged some more ideas of the baseball game we wanted to have. We got home and my mind was just jumping with ideas. I immediately jumped on the computer and started to put together a flyer. I decided to call it "Baseball for Children with Autism." It was a pretty boring and cheesy name but it was all I came up with. Hey, it was late at night and I was tired.

Later that month, my mother and I headed to a health food store with Deets and finally came up with the final name for the event. We were talking about the annual walk that Autism Speaks put on called Walk Now for Autism, and it hit me. I turned to my mom and said, "We should call it 'Play Now'." We exchanged grins and decided to make it official. The event was officially called "Play Now for Autism!"

That next month, the new flyer was designed and ready to go. While in the car going to school, my mom told me that she has a friend, Gloria (remember her, Aric's mom), who wants to help out. I was fine with the idea; the more help we could get, the better. Then she told me that they were thinking of changing the name to "Play Ball for Autism," but I was not hooked on that name. I wanted to keep the whole "now" theme like Walk Now, Ride Now for Autism, Give Now, TACA Now, Cure Autism Now and more. I like the way they all contained the word "now," so I decided to keep it with the original name.

Play Now for Autism was off to a slow start so we decided to really get moving on it in December. Little did we know we were in for a pretty big shock. I was at my grandparent's house on my dad's side and it was the morning just before Christmas Eve when my phone rang. "Zack?" my grandmother said. "Yeah, what happened?" I replied. Then she told me that my great-grandfather had just passed away. I was so surprised; he was the last person I ever expected to go. I then received a call from my cousin, Celina, and she told me what happened. We chatted for a little bit and then I took a deep breath and walked down stairs.

I walked into the kitchen, my cousins were sitting at the table eating breakfast after being dropped off for the day, and my grandma, Lorraine, was cooking. I walked toward her and told her what happened. She looked at me and told me how sorry she was. Then, I just broke down into tears. I then pulled myself together and went back upstairs to think. Then my grandpa walked in and asked me how I felt and asked me if I wanted to go home, but I refused. It was the holiday season and it was just too much for me to go home and deal with all the sorrow.

After a nice Christmas Eve, Christmas morning I was ready to head home. I got home and walked in while everyone was opening their presents. We all opened our gifts and enjoyed the day. Late December we had the funeral services and burial. It was a tough time but after it all finished Play Now was ready to go once again.

It was now mid-January and my mother and I were headed to an Autism Speaks meeting. There we introduced our idea to the rest of the committee members and it was all ready to go. We passed out flyers and had full support from the committee. Later on into February, we did a lot more advertising and I was welcomed into the Autism Speaks family as a committee member for the walk-a-ton in April. I then wrote an article for the newspaper, The Voice, and made speeches at the Walk Now Kick-Off Events.

It was all becoming real. We had the park booked, the flyers done and being passed out, and everything was just falling into place. Then, we met with Lynne from our local councilman's office. She told us that they were going to provide us with the booths, a stage, and other equipment. Everything was going great! The band was good to go, the booth holders and vendors were ready, and volunteers kept pouring in. We had some Dodgers Legends, a petting zoo, and a rock-climbing wall all ready. We had our t-shirts made and it was all looking good. Jay even got us Dodger Dogs donated from Levy Restaurants, where he worked.

Autism Talk Radio

It was the Friday before our big day and I received an email from the host of Autism Talk Radio. He asked me to go on the show to talk about the event and how I got involved with autism. I was so excited. I couldn't wait to do it.

That Saturday, we got the whole interview all set up and I was ready to go on. I was upstairs on my aunt, Monique's, laptop awaiting the phone call to start the live interview. I was so nervous and on the verge of an anxiety attack. Then, I remembered that mom always told me that if I am ever nervous, to take three big deep breathes and try to calm down. The phone rang and this was it. I answered and sure enough it was the host calling asking if I was ready for the over-the-phone interview.

He asked me if there was anything else I wanted to include, aside from Play Now and myself. I told him that I would also like to mention the walk in April. He agreed and then we had begun. It was so crazy. I had never done a live interview before and it was all so unreal. I could not believe what was happening all because of my little idea.

Finally, the show started and the theme song played. Then Steve, the host, introduced me. I was not as nervous as before but instead more excited. Then we right away jumped into the Q&A. We covered topics such as the GFCF Diet and vaccines. I talked a lot about the event and how people can get started on their own event and then we talked more about my family and I. We finished the show with a quick overview of the walk and of all the details of the baseball event. Then, Steve thanked me for being on the show and it was all done.

I was not expecting to be done as quickly as we were but I was kind of happy that it was finally done. Now I had to wait about an hour until it became available to the public. I could not wait to hear how funny I sounded and ready to laugh at what I said and how it went. It actually went pretty well, I was a bit shocked. The only thing was that Amber called right in the middle of it so you can hear where it cuts out when it beeped saying I had a call on the other line. I was a bit funny but overall I think the interview went pretty darn well.

STRESSING OUT!

It was finally the night before Play Now for Autism, and there was still so much to do. We were all running around and trying to get as much done as possible. We were at my great-grandmother's house working on the computer and updating everything. We were already stressed and then Jay walks in. He's stressed out himself and then he came in and wanted to leave already.

We were nowhere close to being done and his nagging was upsetting my mother and I. It ended up turning into a loud argument between the three of us and we were getting nowhere. The three of us all have big mouths and Jay and I especially have pretty big egos and it was not looking good at all. All it did was make us even crazier. We were becoming divided by the minute and then we all came to a conclusion: We needed to work together and communicate better. If we were going to pull this off we needed to make sure we did not clash again: we are a team and we need to stay that way. It was not going to be easy since we were tired and cranky but it was the only way we could get it all ready for tomorrow.

We finally finished and went back to my house to get things situated. Once it was all ready to go, my mom and Jay left and went home. We all went to bed and got up at five in the morning to get started. My mom went to get some last minute things together while Jay and I headed to the park to put up signs and posters. As we waited for Lisa[11] to open the gates to the fields up at Northeast Los Angeles Little League[12], we took a small break and waited in the car.

After she got there, we went in and began setting up what we could until the booths and other equipment arrived. It was all scheduled to come at 9 A.M. and then the first vendor showed up and then the next. It was now 10 A.M. and still no sign of equipment. I was there, wondering what the hell is going on! Then, my phone rang and it was Lynne. "Hey Zack, I know you are probably in a panic-mode right now but there was a problem and the order never fell threw." Panic-mode? Are you joking? I was past panic-mode! The only thing in my mind was, "How the hell did the order not go through?" At this point I am so pissed. She told me that if we would find a place to get the equipment then they would

---

[11] Vice President of Northeast Los Angeles Little League.

[12] The park where Play Now was hosted.

pay us back. Now I'm like a chicken with its head cut off running around.

There are some angry vendors and parking turned into a mad house. It was all crashing down and I was ready to lose my mind. I literally wanted to just cancel the whole thing. I had no idea what to do and then finally my great-uncle, Oscar, calls me up saying that he found us a place and ordered us the tables and chairs for the booths. I was finally relieved and things we slowly starting to fall into place. Our band, The Conductors, arrived and with help from Armando[13] the band was all set (even without a stage).

The volunteers came and the families started flowing in. It was all starting to once again get back on track. The event started, the booths arrived, and we got the first baseball game started. Unfortunately, we ran out of the free shirts that we were giving away to the kids. Luckily, we got a list made of all the families that needed shirts so we could get one to them. Play Now was off to a great start and I could not believe it. I was blown away with the way it all molded together. It had manifested from this small idea, to this huge event.

Shady People

I was surprised to see that everything was going so well. I walked to take a breather and sat down at the Donation Booth that my grandma, Lorraine, was working. She looked at me and told me that my grandpa could not get into the park. "What?!" I said. She said that the entrances were closed off and they would not let him through. He got so upset he drove all the way back home. I don't know what it was or why I had this feeling but something deep inside me told me "Lisa!" And if you remember back in chapter eight, I said that we should always follow our gut instincts, this is a situation where my gut was going crazy. She was a bit upset about having to wake up early and open the park for us and though she

---

[13] Play Now stage manager.

seemed very helpful, something led me to think that it was her who did this.

She wanted us to close down our event at 2 P.M. when we wanted it to end around 4 P.M. We came to an agreement that we would end at 3 P.M. instead. So right away I was hunting for her. I wanted answers and I wanted them NOW. I was searching everywhere for her until finally I found her. "Lisa, why are the entrances closed off?" I asked her. "Well I don't know Zack." she replied. She went on and said that the park rangers probably closed off the park, which seemed a little a bunch of bullshit to me. Why would they close it down at 1 P.M.? Why would they close it down without consulting with anyone else or letting everyone in the park know that it was closing? It didn't make sense but I just kind of blew it off.

I was so upset but it was out of my control. We could have had a much bigger turn out without this sabotage. We had a lot of people (including our own family) call us saying that they could not make it in the park. It was very disappointing. I still never knew for a fact that it really was Lisa but the way I saw it, all fingers pointed at her. It made a lot of sense but at this point I honestly do not know. All I know is that whoever did it had to have a cold heart and had to have some pretty high power (Lisa? She was Vice-President). It had to have been someone who wanted to event over early (Lisa?). I believe in my heart that either she knew about it and did nothing or she had something to do with it because our guts do not give us these instincts for nothing. Even the President of the park, Gabriel, wondered why the event was ending so early.

A SUCCESS AFTER ALL!

After the craziness we continued on and mysteriously, after talking to Lisa, the entrances were re-opened. We went on with the performances and the raffles and concluded with our final game. We thanked everyone and closed shop. We collected all the money, cleaned up, and headed home. We went to my great-grandmother's house with the rest of the family and counted up all the money.

Saving Deets!

We hit an easy $1,000 in $20's alone and another with all the other bills and checks. We came to a grand total of over $2,000. It was a pretty good turnout especially since it didn't have too much prep work done and it was our first year. I wish we could have made a lot more money and we did receive a few other complaints about people who were unable to make it into the park but overall, I think it turned out pretty damn good! We made a nice chunk of change to donate and now we know what to expect for next year.

After Play Now, we received a lot of positive responses and a lot of congrat's. We had a stressful but totally fun time doing it. For once, these kids got a chance to be who they are and play baseball (some for the first time). Even though we did not make $10,000 or more, we still made a lot of children happy. As long as I got a chance to do something good for a cause that I love, it truly is a success after all!

Photograph by Arlene Lopez

Zack Gonzalez

Photograph by Arlene Lopez

Photograph by Arlene Lopez

Saving Deets!

Photograph by Arlene Lopez

Photograph by Arlene Lopez

Photograph by Arlene Lopez

Zack Gonzalez

Photograph by Arlene Lopez

Please note that some of the names in this chapter have been changed or modified for protection purposes

Saving Deets!

Chapter 15:
The Dear Deets Diary

"Together we can conquer the world."

- Zack Gonzalez

Throughout this whole journey with Ethan, there have been many ups and downs. It has literally been a roller coaster and somehow my family and I have gotten the chance to stick through it. Along the way, I wrote a few small notes to Ethan. I have collected them all and decided to create the "Dear Deets Diary." Below are just a few of my "Dear Deets" diary entries so feel free to read my personal thoughts and relate.

"Dear Deets,

I want you to know that even though it may sound like I did not love you, I did. I loved you very much, I was just a little lost. I want you to know that I will always love you and I will always be there for you. I want you to be the best you can be and I will help you become that ultimate best! Together we will conquer the world!"

This Dear Deets was in response to chapter one and how I came off a little cold. This is my explanation to Ethan saying that I do love him, no matter what.

April 30

"Dear Deets,

Today we went to the Dodger game and man was it tough. I could tell that with all the people there it was kind of hard for you to handle. I would be going crazy and acting up if I were you, too. Though once we got in our seats, everything was fine. It gave me a little tear to see that you were actually cheering on the Dodgers. I love you, daddy."

Man was it tough at this game. Ethan was rolling around on the floor and misbehaving. But what really pissed me off was that dumb lady who said that he needed a spanking. My mom told me she said that when I was off with EJ (he caught his first ball!!!!). I got so pissed! My mom gave her one of those cards I mentioned back in the chapter about tantrums. After she got the card from my mom, she went "Hmmp," stuck her nose in the air and kept strutting. If she did that to me, I would have told her to read the card carefully, then research autism, then shoved that card right up her ignorant ass (please excuse my language but if someone said that about your baby, I'm pretty sure you would feel the same way). Sometimes people just need to mind their own damn business.

May 15

"Dear Deets,

Today I did another interview with a man named Sal. You don't know him but he is an Autie-Dad, like your dad. He told me that everyone was proud of me because of the passion that I have for this cause but really Ethan, you are what keeps me going. You are my inspiration!"

When I spoke with Sal, I felt so good. I knew he was going to be a huge help. Even though he talked my ear off for an hour, I knew he would be a big help with the book.

June 1

"Dear Deets,

Today you got home from school and ran into the living room and started play with some flashcards. I was shocked to see that you were reading them. I would get them and show you a card and you would read the word. You paid no attention to the picture, just the word. You make me so proud that you keep progressing. Even though Adam disrupted your thought by sitting on your cards, it's okay because you still did good!"

Ethan was so good at reading. Now, I know he knew how to read some words because I would see him reading his *Thomas ad Friends* books but I was shocked to see that he was not even really bothering to look at the pictures on the card; he just read the words underneath them. And Adam, he's my uncle (FYI).

June 3

"Dear Deets,

Today we were watching *America's Funniest Home Videos*, and you were cracking me up. I was just watching you laugh and scream like crazy. It is your favorite show, and man did I get a kick out of you! You're crazy. I love you!"

He loves to watch that show. He cracks up every time we watch it. He gets so excited that he lets out these little screams. He's too funny.

June 13

"Dear Deets,

Today was your last baseball game! Sorry I showed up late but it was still fun at the barbeque. Though, Tina gave you that big piece of cake and after that you were not into it. You were fussy and thought it was funny spitting and gagging yourself. It was much better later though when we got to my house and were playing with mom on the laptop! I love you!"

It was funny once we got to my house. We jumped on my laptop and went on YouTube and were watching funny clips and videos. Ethan is so funny. We started recording ourselves and then we would go back and watch them. Ah, it was a good day!

June 16

"Dear Deets,

It's the day after my birthday and I just got home and we all got ready and went to go out to eat at Tokyo Wacko. You were being so bad until the chef let up that happy face and you saw that fire. You got so scared, daddy. But afterwards we went out for ice cream and had a pretty good evening."

At Tokyo Wacko they cook the food right in front of you and before they cook the make a happy face and light it on fire as part of their show and Deets got so scared. It made gave me a little smirk. Though I have a funny story to tell about that day. Before we went to eat, we went to buy a cake. The first bakery didn't have parking so we went to the next one and got the cake with "Happy

Birthday Zack" on it and everything but their card machine didn't work and we didn't have cash. It was getting late so I said screw it. I was just going to manage without a cake. Now, the whole time I was thinking of my ideal birthday cake. It would be an ice cream cake made of pure raspberry sorbet. Yum! I had this vision in my head. Then after we ate, instead of getting cake we decided to go at get some ice cream and as I was looking to pick a flavor, I saw raspberry sorbet! I wanted a raspberry sorbet cake so bad that God actually gave me my dream cake. Now, it wasn't exactly a cake but it was an awesome substitute.

July 9

"Dear Deets,

Today I got to meet your chiropractor for the first time. Mom's right, he is like a big kid. He seems pretty cool.

Ethan has the coolest chiropractor. He is so awesome. He has such a welcoming personality. It is hard finding a good chiropractor.

July 12

"Dear Deets,

Today we went to the circus. Despite the screaming and overexcitement, it went pretty well. As first I was a little embarrassed and upset when you would scream and people would tell me to shut you up but after hearing a few other kids scream too, I knew you weren't alone."

Ethan is having an issue with screaming. At first it was when he would get excited or overwhelmed but now I think he just does it to get attention. The circus experience was pretty good. Ethan enjoyed it and afterwards he got a light up toys sword that had sound effects. It was a pretty good day.

July 19

"Dear Deets,

I just want you to always remember that I love you and I will do anything for you. Today we went to the park with your friends Aric, Darnell, Andrew, Nico, Evelyn, and Katelyn. You are so funny. You just love to get rise out of people. You threw sand at Darnell and he almost beat you to pieces. That's what you get daddy, you can't do that. Be good. I love you."

Aric, Darnell, Nico, and Andrew are also autistic. They are Ethan's classmates except Nico. Nico's mom is our family friend, Jeni. We all went to the park. My mom is friends with their moms: Veronica, Gloria, Jeni, and Tina. It was a pretty fun and pretty crazy day. Ethan just loves to get reactions out of people. He threw sand at Darnell and Deets is little compared to Darnell. So I knew he got scared when Darnell was getting ready to hit him.

"Dear Deets,

Today, I finished the book!! Yay! I did it! I mean, WE DID IT! I couldn't have done it without you. Every day you make me more and more proud as I see you make progress more and more. I love you so much! You are the best gift I've ever gotten. You helped me find myself again. You helped me find my voice again. I'm so glad we did this!"

I'm so glad I finally finished the book! It is exciting and crazy just like every day I spend with Ethan. With every day that comes, I always have to be ready for the unexpected. Whether it is freaking out because he is starting to climb on the roof or getting annoyed with his high-pitch screams or tearing as I see and hear him reading a book or laughing watching him do yoga in the morning. He is filled with surprises! He is one of the best gifts God has given me. I have to remember to thank Him every day for giving me such a beautiful life.

August: Summer Camp Days

"Dear Deets,

These past two weeks I spent with you at summer camp have been great. It reminded me why I love doing what I do, and that is advocate. I got to spend time with you and all the other special needs children and those were my best days of summer. I can't wait until next year"

I spent a few days at summer camp with Deets this summer and it was great. It really opened my eyes to see how special these kids are. It has also opened my eyes to see how much special needs kids are just kind of pushed off to the side and left out by "typical" kids and sometimes other adults. Luckily Ethan's camp councilors were great. And Deborah, oh Deb, she was in charge of the special needs group. She was awesome! Much respect to her. For you readers, I highly recommend sending your kids there. It is the Anderson Summer Camp at the Rose Bowl Aquatics Center in Pasadena, CA.

Saving Deets!

Chapter 16:
Saving Deets…

"With everyday, a new journey begins."

- **Zack Gonzalez**

T his has been a constant struggle. With everyday a new journey begins. Ethan is not free of autism. He is not cured. He is recovering little by little but I still love him the way he is. If it weren't for him, I wouldn't have written this book. I wouldn't have created Play Now. I wouldn't have been volunteering. I thank him because he is the reason I am doing this. With Help from God, Ethan is my main inspiration.

This journey is not yet over. There is still so much more we have to experience. So let me just spill it now: this is not the last time you will hear from me. Ethan is still a kid. There are going to be so many stories in his teenage years and in his adult years when he goes to prom and when he graduates and gets married (I'm tearing up as I write this). This journey is a life-long journey and I plan on living it out! God gave us Ethan for a reason. Was it because He knew I would write this book? Maybe. Was it because He knew my family would be so involved? Maybe. I don't know why but I do know that no matter what I am going to make Him proud. He is always there for me and if there was one thing I want Ethan to never lose, it is his faith. If there were any advice I could give, it would be to always appreciate what you have; see everything as a blessing and never a curse. It may be negative but you can always make it positive. If we always see that God or the world is cursing us then we will never be blessed.

So, this is our journey so far in *Saving Deets!*

Saving Deets!

VACCINE CHARTS

It is very important to know what goes into our bodies. When we get vaccinated there are so many toxins and metals. Some vaccines are pretty unhealthy. To help you out I have included a few very important charts obtained from Generation Rescue, the FDA (US Food & Drug Administration), and the CDC (Center of Disease Control).

Vaccine Excipient & Media Summary, Part 2
Excipients Included in U.S. Vaccines, by Vaccine

Includes vaccine ingredients (e.g., adjuvants and preservatives) as well as substances used during the manufacturing process,
including vaccine-production media, that are removed from the final product and present only in trace quantities.
In addition to the substances listed, most vaccines contain Sodium Chloride (table salt).

Vaccines	Ingredients*
By multiple manufacturers	partial list in one or more vaccines
Anthrax (BioThrax)	Aluminum Hydroxide, Amino Acids, Benzethonium Chloride, Formaldehyde or Formalin, Inorganic Salts and Sugars, Vitamins
BCG (Tice)	Asparagine, Citric Acid, Lactose, Glycerin, Iron Ammonium Citrate, Magnesium Sulfate, Potassium Phosphate
DTaP (Daptacel)	Aluminum Phosphate, Ammonium Sulfate, Casamino Acid, Dimethyl-betacyclodextrin, Formaldehyde or Formalin, Glutaraldehyde, 2-Phenoxyethanol
DTaP (Infanrix)	Aluminum Hydroxide, Bovine Extract, Formaldehyde or Formalin, Glutaraldhyde, 2-Phenoxyethanol, Polysorbate 80
DTaP (Tripedia)	Aluminum Potassium Sulfate, Ammonium Sulfate, Bovine Extract, Formaldehyde or Formalin, Gelatin, Polysorbate 80, Sodium Phosphate, Thimerosal*
DTaP/Hib (TriHIBit)	Aluminum Potassium Sulfate, Ammonium Sulfate, Bovine Extract, Formaldehyde or Formalin, Gelatin, Polysorbate 80, Sucrose, Thimerosal*
DTaP-IPV (Kinrix)	Aluminum Hydroxide, Bovine Extract, Formaldehyde, Lactalbumin Hydrolysate, Monkey Kidney Tissue, Neomycin Sulfate, Polymyxin B, Polysorbate 80

Vaccines	Ingredients*
By multiple manufacturers	partial list in one or more vaccines
DTaP-HepB-IPV (Pediarix)	Aluminum Hydroxide, Aluminum Phosphate, Bovine Protein, Lactalbumin
	Hydrolysate, Formaldehyde or Formalin, Glutaraldhyde, Monkey Kidney
	Tissue, Neomycin, 2-Phenoxyethanol, Polymyxin B, Polysorbate 80, Yeast Protein
DtaP-IPV/Hib (Pentacel)	Aluminum Phosphate, Bovine Serum Albumin, Formaldehyde, Glutaraldehyde,
	MRC-5 DNA and Cellular Protein, Neomycin, Polymyxin B Sulfate,
	Polysorbate 80, 2-Phenoxyethanol,
DT (sanofi)	Aluminum Potassium Sulfate, Bovine Extract, Formaldehyde or Formalin,
	Thimerosal (multi-dose) or Thimerosal* (single-dose)
DT (Massachusetts)	Aluminum Hydroxide, Formaldehyde or Formalin
Hib (ACTHib)	Ammonium Sulfate, Formaldehyde or Formalin, Sucrose
Hib (PedvaxHib)	Aluminum Hydroxyphosphate Sulfate
Hib/Hep B (Comvax)	Amino Acids, Aluminum Hydroxyphosphate Sulfate, Dextrose, Formaldehyde
	or Formalin, Mineral Salts, Sodium Borate, Soy Peptone, Yeast Protein
Hep A (Havrix)	Aluminum Hydroxide, Amino Acids, Formaldehyde or Formalin, MRC-5
	Cellular Protein, Neomycin Sulfate, 2-Phenoxyethanol, Phosphate Buffers,
	Polysorbate
Hep A (Vaqta)	Aluminum Hydroxyphosphate Sulfate, Bovine Albumin or Serum, DNA,
	Formaldehyde or Formalin, MRC-5 Cellular Protein, Sodium Borate
Hep B (Engerix-B)	Aluminum Hydroxide, Phosphate Buffers, Thimerosal*, Yeast Protein
Hep B (Recombivax)	Aluminum Hydroxyphosphate Sulfate, Amino Acids, Dextrose, Formaldehyde
	or Formalin, Mineral Salts, Potassium Aluminum Sulfate, Soy Peptone, Yeast Protein

Vaccines	Ingredients*
By multiple manufacturers	partial list in one or more vaccines
HepA/HepB (Twinrix)	Aluminum Hydroxide, Aluminum Phosphate, Amino Acids, Dextrose,
	Formaldehyde or Formalin, Inorganic Salts, MRC-5 Cellular Protein, Neomycin
	Sulfate, 2-Phenoxyethanol, Phosphate Buffers, Polysorbate 20, Thimerosal*,
	Vitamins, Yeast Protein
Human Papillomavirus (HPV) (Gardasil)	Amino Acids, Amorphous Aluminum Hydroxyphosphate Sulfate,
	Carbohydrates, L-histidine, Mineral Salts, Polysorbate 80, Sodium Borate,
	Vitamins
Influenza (Afluria)	Beta-Propiolactone, Calcium Chloride, Neomycin, Ovalbumin, Polymyxin B,
	Potassium Chloride, Potassium Phosphate, Sodium Phosphate, Sodium
	Taurodeoxychoalate.
Influenza (Fluarix)	Egg Albumin (Ovalbumin), Egg Protein, Formaldehyde or Formalin,
	Gentamicin, Hydrocortisone, Octoxynol-10, á-Tocopheryl Hydrogen Succinate,
	Polysorbate 80, Sodium Deoxycholate, Sodium Phosphate, Thimerosal*
Influenza (Flulaval)	Egg Albumin (Ovalbumin), Egg Protein, Formaldehyde or Formalin, Sodium
	Deoxycholate, Phosphate Buffers, Thimerosal
Influenza (Fluvirin)	Beta-Propiolactone , Egg Protein, Neomycin, Polymyxin B, Polyoxyethylene 9-
	10 Nonyl Phenol (Triton N-101, Octoxynol 9), Thimerosal (multidose
	containers), Thimerosal* (single-dose syringes)
Influenza (Fluzone)	Egg Protein, Formaldehyde or Formalin, Gelatin, Octoxinol-9 (Triton X-100),
	Thimerosal (multidose containers)
Influenza (FluMist)	Chick Kidney Cells, Egg Protein, Gentamicin Sulfate, Monosodium Glutamate,
	Sucrose Phosphate Glutamate Buffer

Vaccines	Ingredients*
By multiple manufacturers	partial list in one or more vaccines
IPV (Ipol)	Calf Serum Protein, Formaldehyde or Formalin, Monkey Kidney Tissue,
	Neomycin, 2-Phenoxyethanol, Polymyxin B, Streptomycin,
Japanese Encephalitis (JE-Vax)	Formaldehyde or Formalin, Gelatin, Mouse Serum Protein, Polysorbate 80,
	Thimerosal
Japanese Encephalitis (Ixiaro)	Aluminum Hydroxide, Bovine Serum Albumin, Formaldehyde, Protamine
	Sulfate, Sodium Metabisulphite
Meningococcal (Menactra)	Formaldehyde or Formalin, Phosphate Buffers
Meningococcal (Menomune)	Lactose, Thimerosal (10-dose vials only)
MMR (MMR-II)	Amino Acid, Bovine Albumin or Serum, Chick Embryo Fibroblasts, Human
	Serum Albumin, Gelatin, Glutamate, Neomycin, Phosphate Buffers, Sorbitol,
	Sucrose, Vitamins
MMRV (ProQuad)	Bovine Albumin or Serum, Gelatin, Human Serum Albumin, Monosodium Lglutamate,
	MRC-5 Cellular Protein, Neomycin, Sodium Phosphate Dibasic,
	Sodium Bicarbonate, Sorbitol, Sucrose, Potassium Phosphate Monobasic,
	Potassium Chloride, Potassium Phosphate Dibasic
Pneumococcal (Pneumovax)	Bovine Protein, Phenol
Pneumococcal (Prevnar)	Aluminum Phosphate, Amino Acid, Soy Peptone, Yeast Extract
Rabies (Imovax)	Human Serum Albumin, Beta-Propiolactone, MRC-5 Cellular Protein,
	Neomycin, Phenol Red (Phenolsulfonphthalein), Vitamins
Rabies (RabAvert)	Amphotericin B, Beta-Propiolactone, Bovine Albumin or Serum, Chicken
	Protein, Chlortetracycline, Egg Albumin (Ovalbumin), Ethylenediamine-
	Tetraacetic Acid Sodium (EDTA), Neomycin, Potassium Glutamate

Vaccines	Ingredients*
By multiple manufacturers	partial list in one or more vaccines
Rotavirus (RotaTeq)	Cell Culture Media, Fetal Bovine Serum, Sodium Citrate, Sodium Phosphate
	Monobasic Monohydrate, Sodium Hydroxide Sucrose, Polysorbate 80
Rotavirus (Rotarix)	Amino Acids, Calcium Carbonate, Calcium Chloride, D-glucose, Dextran,
	Ferric (III) Nitrate, L-cystine, L-tyrosine, Magnesium Sulfate, Phenol Red,
	Potassium Chloride, Sodium Hydrogenocarbonate, Sodium Phosphate, Sodium
	L-glutamine, Sodium Pyruvate, Sorbitol, Sucrose, Vitamins, Xanthan
Td (Decavac)	Aluminum Potassium Sulfate, Bovine Extract, Formaldehyde or Formalin, 2-
	Phenoxyethanol, Peptone, Thimerosal*
Td (Massachusetts)	Aluminum Hydroxide, Aluminum Phosphate, Formaldehyde or Formalin,
	Thimerosal (some multidose containers)
Tdap (Adacel)	Aluminum Phosphate, Formaldehyde or Formalin, Glutaraldehyde, 2-
	Phenoxyethanol
Tdap (Boostrix)	Aluminum Hydroxide, Bovine Extract, Formaldehyde or Formalin,
	Glutaraldehyde, Polysorbate 80
Typhoid (inactivated – Typhim Vi)	Disodium Phosphate, Monosodium Phosphate, Phenol, Polydimethylsilozone,
	Hexadecyltrimethylammonium Bromide
Typhoid (oral – Ty21a)	Am ino Acids, Ascorbic Acid, Bovine Protein, Casein, Dextrose, Galactose,
	Gelatin, Lactose, Magnesium Stearate, Sucrose, Yeast Extract
Vaccinia (ACAM2000)	Glycerin, Human Serum Albumin, Mannitol, Monkey Kidney Cells, Neomycin,
	Phenol, Polymyxin B

Vaccines	Ingredients*
By multiple manufacturers	partial list in one or more vaccines
Varicella (Varivax)	Bovine Albumin or Serum, Ethylenediamine-Tetraacetic Acid Sodium (EDTA),
	Gelatin, Monosodium L-Glutamate, MRC-5 DNA and Cellular Protein,
	Neomycin, Potassium Chloride, Potassium Phosphate Monobasic, Sodium
	Phosphate Monobasic, Sucrose
Yellow Fever (YF-Vax)	Egg Protein, Gelatin, Sorbitol
Zoster (Zostavax)	Bovine Calf Serum, Hydrolyzed Porcine Gelatin, Monosodium L-glutamate,
	MRC-5 DNA and Cellular Protein, Neomycin, Potassium Phosphate
	Monobasic, Potassium Chloride, Sodium Phosphate Dibasic, Sucrose

April 2009

*Where "thimerosal" is marked with an asterisk (*) it indicates that the product should be considered equivalent to
thimerosal-free products. This vaccine may contain trace amounts (<0.3 mcg) of mercury left after post-production
thimerosal removal, but these amounts have no biological effect. *JAMA* 1999;282(18) and *JAMA* 2000;283(16)
Adapted from Grabenstein JD. *ImmunoFacts: Vaccines & Immunologic Drugs*. St. Louis, MO: Wolters Kluwer
Health Inc.; 2009 and individual products' package inserts.
All reasonable efforts have been made to ensure the accuracy of this information, but manufacturers may change
product contents before that information is reflected here.

Information obtained from:

http://www.cdc.gov/vaccines/pubs/pinkbook/downloads/appendices/B/excipient-table-2.pdf

Below is another chart that includes some possible side effects of certain vaccines.

Pediatric Vaccine Ingredients and Possible Side Effects

Vaccines By multiple manufacturers	Ingredients* partial list in one or more vaccines	Side Effects** including a partial list of reactions, events & reports*
DTaP (Diptheria, Tetanus, Toxiods, and Acellular Pertussis) Vaccine Absorbed	Aluminum Phosphate, Ammonium Sulfate, Aluminum Potassium Sulfate, Thimerosal [a vaccine preservative that is approximately 50% mercury by weight] Formaldehyde or Formalin, Glutaraldehye, 2-Phoenoxyethanol, Dimethyl-betacyclodextrin, Sodium Phosphate, Polysorbate 80.	Autism, fever, anorexia, vomiting, pneumonia, meningitis, sepsis, pertussis, convulsions, febrile, grand mal, afebrile and partial seizures, encephalopathy, brachial neuritis, Guillain-Barré syndrome, Sudden Infant Death syndrome.
DTaP/HepB/IPV Combination Vaccine, Diphtheria and Tetanus Toxoids and Acellular Pertusis Adsorbed, Hepatitis B (Recombinant) and Inactivated Poliovirus Vaccine Combined	Aluminum Hydroxide, Aluminum Phosphate, Formaldehyde or Formalin, Glutaraldhyde, Monkey Kidney Tissue, Neomycin, 2-Phenoxyethanol, Polymyxin B, Polysorbate 80, Antibiotics, Yeast Protein.	Seizures, diabetes mellitus, asthma, Sudden Infant Death Syndrome, upper respiratory tract infection, abnormal liver function tests, anorexia, jaundice, shock, encephalopathy, Stevens-Johnson syndrome, brachial neuritis.
Flu Vaccine Influenza Virus Vaccine	Thimerosal [a preservative that is approximately 50% mercury by weight], Chick Kidney Cells, Egg Protein, Gentamicin Sulfate, Antibiotics, Monosodium Glutamate [MSG], Sucrose Phosphate Glutamate Buffer.	Significant respiratory and gastrointestinal symptoms, seizure, allergic asthma , decreased appetite, increased mitochondrial encephalomyopathy, partial facial paralysis, Guillain-Barré syndrome, Bell's palsy, Stevens-Johnson syndrome, herpes zoster [shingles].

Vaccines By multiple manufacturers	Ingredients* partial list in one or more vaccines	Side Effects** including a partial list of reactions, events & reports*
Hep B Vaccine Hepatitis B Vaccine	Aluminum Hydroxyphosphate Sulfate, Amino Acids, Dextrose, Phosphate Buffers, Potassium Aluminum Sulfate, Formaldehyde or Formalin, Mineral Salts, Soy Peptone, Yeast Protein	Influenza, febrile seizure, anorexia, upper respiratory tract illnesses, herpes zoster, encephalitis, palpitations, arthritis, systemic lupus erthematosus (SLE), conjunctivitis, abnormal liver function tests, Guillain-Barré syndrome, Bell's palsy, multiple sclerosis, anaphylaxis, seizures.
HIB Vaccine Haemophilus b Conjugate Vaccine (Tetanus Toxiod Conjugate)	Ammonium Sulfate, Formaldehyde or Formalin, Sucrose.	Anorexia, seizures, renal failure, Guillain-Barré Syndrome (GBS), diarrhea, vomiting.
HIB/HepB Vaccine (Recombinant) Haemophilus b Conjugate (Meningococcal Protein Conjugate) and Hep B	Aluminum Hydroxyphosphate Sulfate, Formaldehyde or Formalin, Sodium Borate, Soy Peptone, Yeast Protein, AminoAcids, Dextrose, Mineral Salts.	Anorexia, seizure, otitis media [ear infections], upper respiratory infection, oral candidasis [yeast infection], anaphylaxis [shock].
HIB / Meningococcal [Haemophilus b Conjugate Vaccine (Meningococcal Protein Conjugate)]	Aluminum Hydroxyphosphate Sulfate, Formaldehyde or Formalin, Phosphate Buffers.	Febrile seizures, early onset HIB disease, otitis media [ear infection], upper respiratory infection, Guillain-Barré syndrome.
MMR Vaccine Measles, Mumps and Rubella Virus Vaccine Live	Chick Embryo Fibroblasts, Amino Acid, Bovine Albumin or Serum, Human Serum Albumin, Antibiotics, Glutamate, Phosphate Buffers, Gelatin, Sorbitol, Sucrose, Vitamins.	Atypical measles, arthritis, encephalitis, death, aseptic meningitis, nerve deafness, otitis media [ear infection].

Vaccines By multiple manufacturers	Ingredients* partial list in one or more vaccines	Side Effects** including a partial list of reactions, events & reports*
Pneumococcal Pneumococcal 7-valent Conjugate Vaccine (Diphtheria CRM197 Protein)	Aluminum Phosphate, Yeast Extract, Amino Acid, Soy Peptone.	Febrile seizure, Sudden Infant Death, anaphylactiod reaction including shock, decreased appetite,
Poliovirus Vaccine (IPV) Poliovirus Vaccine Inactivated	2-Phenoxyethanol, Formaldehyde or Formalin, Monkey Kidney Tissue, Newborn Calf Serum Protein, Antibiotics, Neomycin, Polymyxin B, Streptomycin.	Death, anorexia, Guillain-Barré syndrome.
Chicken Pox (Varicella) Virus Vaccine	Ethylenediamine-Tetraacetic Acid Sodium (EDTA) [a metals chelation agent], Bovine Albumin or Serum, Antibiotics, Monosodium glutamate [MSG], MRC-5 DNA and Cellular Protein, Neomycin, Potassium Chloride, Potassium Phosphate Monobasic, Sodium Phosphate Monobasic,Sucrose.	Febrile seizures, encephalitis, Varicella-like rash, upper respiratory illness, lower respiratory illness, eczema, encephalitis, facial edema, cold/canker sore, aseptic meningitis, Guillain-Barré Syndrome, Bell's palsy, pneumonia, secondary bacterial infections.

- **A partial ingredient list from *Vaccine Excipient & Media Summary, Part 2, Excipients included in U.S. Vaccines, by Vaccine*. Downloaded 11/08 from:** www.cdc.gov/vaccines/pubs/pinkbook/downloads/appendices/B/excipient-table-2.pdf

** This list contains a combination of many adverse post-vaccination occurrences, and possible occurrences, that have been published in the manufacturer's documents. Any use of [brackets] is information added by the author. This list may not contain all the adverse occurrences; it may contain typographical errors, and obviously does not take the place of reading the most current manufacturer's document in its entirety.

Zack Gonzalez

Information obtained from:

http://www.generationrescue.org/vaccine_information/

Below is another chart. This chart includes the amount of thimerosal and mercury.

Thimerosal and Expanded List of Vaccines

– (updated 3/14/2008)
Thimerosal Content in Currently Manufactured U.S. Licensed Vaccines

Vaccine	Trade Name	Manufacturer	Thimerosal Concentration[1]	Mercury
Anthrax	Anthrax vaccine	Emergent BioDefense Operations Lansing Inc.	0	0
DTaP	Tripedia[2]	Sanofi Pasteur, Inc	≤ 0.00012%	≤ 0.3 µg/0.5 mL dose
	Infanrix	GlaxoSmithKline Biologicals	0	0
	Daptacel	Sanofi Pasteur, Ltd	0	0
DTaP-HepB-IPV	Pediarix	GlaxoSmithKline Biologicals	0	0
DT	No Trade Name	Sanofi Pasteur, Inc	< 0.00012% (single dose)	< 0.3 µg/0.5mL dose
		Sanofi Pasteur, Ltd[3]	0.01%	25 µg/0.5 mL dose

189

Vaccine	Trade Name	Manufacturer	Thimerosal Concentration[1]	Mercury
Td	No Trade Name	Mass Public Health	0.0033%	8.3 µg/0.5 mL dose
	Decavac	Sanofi Pasteur, Inc	≤ 0.00012%	≤ 0.3 µg mercury/0.5 ml dose
	No Trade Name	Sanofi Pasteur, Ltd	0	0
Tdap	Adacel	Sanofi Pasteur, Ltd	0	0
	Boostrix	GlaxoSmithKline Biologicals	0	0
TT	No Trade Name	Sanofi Pasteur, Inc	0.01%	25 µg/0.5 mL dose
Hib	ActHIB/OmniHIB[4]	Sanofi Pasteur, SA	0	0
	HibTITER	Wyeth Pharmaceuticals, Inc.	0	0
	PedvaxHIB liquid	Merck & Co, Inc	0	0
Hib/HepB	COMVAX[5]	Merck & Co, Inc	0	0
Hepatitis B	Engerix-B Pediatric/adolescent Adult	GlaxoSmithKline Biologicals	0 0	0 0
	Recombivax HB Pediatric/adolescent Adult (adolescent) Dialysis	Merck & Co, Inc	0 0 0	0 0 0

Vaccine	Trade Name	Manufacturer	Thimerosal Concentration[1]	Mercury
Hepatitis A	Havrix	GlaxoSmithKline Biologicals	0	0
	Vaqta	Merck & Co, Inc	0	0
HepA/HepB	Twinrix	GlaxoSmithKline Biologicals	< 0.0002%	< 1 μg/1mL dose
IPV	IPOL	Sanofi Pasteur, SA	0	0
	Poliovax	Sanofi Pasteur, Ltd	0	0
Influenza	Afluria	CSL Limited	0 (single dose) 0.01% (multidose)	0/0.5 mL (single dose) 24.5 μg/0.5 mL (multidose)
	Fluzone[6]	Sanofi Pasteur, Inc	0.01%	25 μg/0.5 mL dose
	Fluvirin	Novartis Vaccines and Diagnostics Ltd	0.01%	25 μg/0.5 ml dose
	Fluzone (no thimerosal)	Sanofi Pasteur, Inc	0	0
	Fluvirin (Preservative Free)	Novartis Vaccines and Diagnostics Ltd	< 0.0004%	< 1 μg/0.5 mL dose
	Fluarix	GlaxoSmithKline Biologicals	< 0.0004%	< 1 μg/0.5 ml dose
	FluLaval	ID Biomedical Corporation of Quebec	0.01%	25 μg/0.5 ml dose

Vaccine	Trade Name	Manufacturer	Thimerosal Concentration[1]	Mercury
Influenza, live	FluMist	MedImmune Vaccines, Inc	0	0
Japanese Encephalitis[7]	JE-VAX	Research Foundation for Microbial Diseases of Osaka University	0.007%	35 µg/1.0mL dose 17.5 µg/0.5 mL dose
MMR	MMR-II	Merck & Co, Inc	0	0
Meningococcal	Menomune A, C, AC and A/C/Y/W-135	Sanofi Pasteur, Inc	0.01% (multidose) 0 (single dose)	25 µg/0.5 dose 0
	Menactra A, C, Y and W-135	Sanofi Pasteur, Inc	0	0
Pneumococcal	Prevnar (Pneumo Conjugate)	Wyeth Pharmaceuticals Inc	0	0
	Pneumovax 23	Merck & Co, Inc	0	0
Rabies	IMOVAX	Sanofi Pasteur, SA	0	0
	Rabavert	Novartis Vaccines and Diagnostics	0	0
Smallpox (Vaccinia), Live	ACAM2000	Acambis, Inc.	0	0
Typhoid Fever	Typhim Vi	Sanofi Pasteur, SA	0	0
	Vivotif	Berna Biotech, Ltd	0	0
Varicella	Varivax	Merck & Co, Inc	0	0
Yellow Fever	Y-F-Vax	Sanofi Pasteurr, Inc	0	0

Zack Gonzalez

Information obtained from:

www.fda.gov/cber/vaccine/Thimerosal.htm#t3

Childcare and School Immunization Requirements

Exemptions Allowed (2007-2008)

Project	Medical		Religious	Philosophical
	Temporary	Permanent		
Alabama		X	X	
Alaska		X	X	
Arizona	X	X	**	*
Arkansas	X		X	X
California	X	X	X	X
Colorado	X	X	X	X

Saving Deets!

Project	Medical		Religious	Philosophical
	Temporary	Permanent		
Connecticut		X	X	
Delaware	X	X	X	
District of Columbia	X	X	X	
Florida	X	X	X	
Georgia	X		X	
Hawaii	X	X	X	
Idaho	X	X	X	X
Illinois		X	X	
Indiana^	X	X	X	
Iowa	X	X	X	
Kansas	X		X	
Kentucky	X	X	X	
Louisiana	X	X	X	X
Maine	X		X	X
Maryland	X	X	X	
Massachusetts	X	X	X	
Michigan	X	X	X	X
Minnesota	X	X	X	X
Mississippi	X	X		
Missouri		X	*	**
Montana	X	X	X	
Nebraska	X	X	X	**
Nevada	X	X	X	
New Hampshire	X		X	
New Jersey	X	X	X	
New Mexico	X	X	X	X
New York	X	X	X	

Project	Medical		Religious	Philosophical
	Temporary	Permanent		
North Carolina	X	X	X	
North Dakota		X	X	X
Ohio	X	X	X	X
Oklahoma	X	X	X	X
Oregon	X	X	X	
Pennsylvania	X	X	X	
Rhode Island	X	X	X	
South Carolina	X	X	X	
South Dakota		X	X	
Tennessee	X	X	X	
Texas	X	X	X	X
Utah	X	X	X	X
Vermont	X	X	X	X
Virginia	X	X	X	
Washington	X	X	X	X
West Virginia	X	X		
Wisconsin	X	X	X	X
Wyoming	X	X	X	

X Exemption allowed
* Allowed in schools only
** Allowed in childcare and head start facilities only
^ Medical exemptions are referred to as "Acute" and "Chronic"

Information obtained from

CDC: http://www2a.cdc.gov/nip/schoolsurv/irExemptions.htm

Here is a list of guidelines according to DAN!

DAN! (Defeat Autism NOW!) Vaccination Guidelines:

1. Use Thimersol / Mercury free vaccines!!
The only way to know for sure a vaccine is mercury/thimersol free is to
read the insert yourself! Many doctors still have mercury/thimersol
vaccines sitting in the refrigerators! And yes, mercury /thimersol
containing vaccines are still being made!! Be sure to be 100% sure!

2. Do not vaccinate newborns.

3. Avoid re-immunization with a vaccine after a previous bad reaction.

4. NEVER vaccinate ill children or children recovering from an infection.

5. Space vaccines - do not give multiple vaccines in 1 day.
(THAT INCLUDES vaccines that have multiple viruses! Split them up!)

6. Use single dose vials from which to draw up the vaccines as opposed
to multiple-dose vials which provide less uniform dosage.

7. Use inactivated polio. (the shot, not the drops)

8. Give RDA (Recommended Daily Allowances) of Vitamin C before and

after vaccines

9. Give a natural form of Vitamin A (cod liver oil) to keep RDA's at

level at all times for the age.

10. Separate the MMR into 3...start with measles at 12-15 months, then

mumps at 18-21 months, rubella at 24-27 months.

11. Do not give live virus vaccines to immunodeficient children.

12. Do not give vaccines if allergic to any of these components:

i. Yeast - Hep B

ii. Eggs - MMR

iii. Neonycian - MMR or Varicella

13. Hold off on the Varicella until 10-12 years & if the child is shown not

immune to Chicken pox.

14. Checking vaccine titers before giving boosters (Most people are

immune after one dose. We continue to get multiple doses that MAY NOT BE NEEDED. Have them check antibody levels via titres blood

test.)

List obtained from: http://generationrescue.org/pdf/vaccine_guidelines.pdf

Some of this information may be hard to understand but just follow the footnotes, Google some stuff, and use Dictionary.com and that should help (that's what I did). Also, remember to check the mercury and thimerosal levels and check all the side effects. This will be very useful come time to vaccinate.

Saving Deets!

Resources

HELPFUL BOOK & WEBSITES

Below are some helpful books and websites that I used to get some of my information. They are all great sources. Some of them may be used for more than one category.

Acceptance

www.autismspeaks.org

Aromatherapy

www.maapservices.org

Autism

www.autism.com

Biomedical Research

www.stankurtz.com

DAN! (Defeating Autism Now!)

www.defeatingautismnow.com

GFCF Diet

www.gfcfmeals.com

www.gfcfdoneeasy.com

http://gfcf-diet.talkaboutcuringautism.org/

http://www.stankurtz.com/biomedical/diet-autism-adhd-chronic-illness.html

Hope

www.amliastarr.com

Raising Brandon - Amalia Starr

Saving Deets!

Mother Warriors - Jenny McCarthy

Louder Than Words - Jenny McCarthy

Organics Foods

www.wholefoods.com

www.ecos.com

www.greenpeople.org/heathfoods.htm

Recovery

www.generationrescue.com

Healing and Preventing Autism - Jenny McCarthy and Jerry Kartzinel M.D.

Special Carbohydrate Diet (SCD)

www.scdiet.org

http://www.stankurtz.com/biomedical/diet-autism-adhd-chronic-illness.html

Vaccines

www.fourteenstudies.org

www.ageofautism.com

www.generationrescue.org

What Your Doctor May Not Tell You About Children's Vaccinations - Stephanie Cave

A Shot In The Dark - Harris Coulter

The Vaccine Guide: Risks and Benefits for Children and Adults - Randall Neustaeder

Vitamins & Supplements

www.brainchildnutritionals.com

www.kartnerhealth.com

www.klaire.com

www.kirkmanlabs.com

For peer support you can find a Rescue Angels. Rescue Angels are those that have had success with recovery. It is free to find a Rescue Angel. They are available in over 38 countries. To find a Rescue Angels use the link provided.

http://www.generationrescue.org/angels.php

About the Author

Zack Gonzalez is a young advocate for autism. He has been involved in the autism community ever since his brother was diagnosed back in 2005. He has made motivational speeches and attends a variety of autism charity events. He has even conducted his own event: Play Now for Autism. He currently lives in Los Angeles, California.

The author will donate a portion of his proceeds to a variety of autism organizations that will help fund for research and help other families.